From the acclaimed author of *A Short History of a Small Place* and *Seaworthy* comes a wholesale departure -- a comic/horror/ romance/fantasy infested with both unsavory American politicians and venomous Venetian lizards. Awash in Pearson's singular wit, *Red Scare* tells the headlong story of a public school biology teacher and a National Gallery curator who join forces to thwart the dire consequences of a medieval Italian curse. This novel, though slender, is packed to overflowing with priapic senators, clueless teenagers, dubious art history, clumsy quasi-romantic repartee, garish worldwide bloodletting, corrosive humor, and enough malicious scuttling reptiles to keep you from ever planting your bare feet on a darkened floor again.

We're pleased to offer *Red Scare* at a special thanks-for-your-ongoing-support price.

Red Scare

Also by T. R. Pearson

Fiction

A Short History of a Small Place
Off For the Sweet Hereafter
The Last of How It Was
Call and Response
Gospel Hour
Cry Me a River
Blue Ridge
Polar
True Cross
Glad News of the Natural World

Nonfiction

Seaworthy: Adrift with William Willis in the Golden Age of Rafting
Augie's Quest **(with Augie Nieto)**

RED SCARE

A NOVEL OF VENOMOUS INTRIGUE

T.R. PEARSON

BARKING MAD PRESS

ISBN – 978-0-615-22750-4

1

The Venetian lagoon shimmers in the dazzling midday sun. It swarms with ferries, barges, water buses, and puny brightly painted police boats that ride low at the gunwales and dart jauntily about. Gondoliers pole and paddle their fares out of gloomy side canals into the blinding light of the San Marco basin. Slender and funereal, the craft bob violently on the chop.

The Piazza San Marco is infested with tourists. On the molo, at the waterfront, they soak up the Adriatic sun, crowding the benches and lounging on the pedestals of the towering twin columns at the water's edge.

Few seats remain at the tables before Cafe Florian where aproned waiters rush about delivering coffee and pastries. At Cafe Quadri, across the square, the band plays selections from *Cats*.

The clock tower, adjacent to the basilica, has attracted a crowd at its base. The clockwork Moors emerge haltingly from their niches on either side of the massive bronze bell. Each carries an upraised hammer in hand. They begin to strike the noon hour, laboriously delivering alternating blows. In the Venetian way, they are quite late.

Tourists stand in a line that works its way toward an entrance to the Palazzo Ducale at the eastern border of the Piazza. It snakes in through the Porta della Carta to the ticket booth beyond. In the grand inner courtyard, visitors tromp up and down the Giants' Stairway where the doges were crowned with their zogias -- their oddly pointed, jewel-encrusted caps. Once properly inside the palace, the tourists follow an unguided route through opulent ante-rooms, into the armory with its collection

7

of military wares, and out across the Bridge of Sighs to the prison, dank and murky in the half-light.

The way out leads through modest, spartan chambers and, unexpectedly, into the cavernous assembly hall where the rhythmic clanging of the clock bell is audible through the filigreed windows. Depicted in a frieze of paintings, high against the assembly hall ceiling, are the first seventy-six doges of Venice. They are elderly hatchet-faced men, each nearly indistinguishable from the others. Oddly, though, one likeness has been painted over with a blackened veil.

Painted onto the veil in flowing golden script are the words --

Hic est locus Marini Faledri decapitati pro criminibus

--Here is the place of Marino Falieri beheaded for his crimes.

In the inner courtyard, at the base of the Giants' Stairway, lies an ancient drainage grate, fashioned from a marble tile. As the clock bell falls silent in the piazza, there is a stirring beneath the grate--dry, raspy, abrupt.

The foot of a lizard reaches into view. A second foot follows. Then the head. The eyes are a searing, luminescent yellow. The creature emerges fully onto the grate. It is no more than eight inches long from tip to tip, unexceptional for an Adriatic skink. Its color, however, is an utterly unnatural, nearly vibrating shade of red. Venetian red.

Another lizard climbs out to join it. Then another. And another, until there are ten scarlet lizards crowding the grate. They attract the notice of a young man, a plump German from Cologne who, weary with sightseeing, has fallen behind his group. He approaches the grate and is dazzled by what he finds. Brilliant red skinks. He's never seen anything like them. One scurries forward, stopping just shy of the toe of his shoe.

Its gullet distends. Its jaws hinge open. It hisses. The racket is remarkably loud. Like steam from a pipe. The sound echoes throughout the courtyard.

The young man chuckles with surprised laughter. He raises his camera to snap a picture. He squats low for a better angle on the lizard at his feet. It parts its jaws. It spits.

A milky splatter coats the camera lens. Cloudy venom splashes onto the young man's fingers and his cheeks. He stands upright, struggling already for breath. He would cry out if he could. His muscles contract and stiffen. His eyes burn intolerably.

The scarlet lizards dart and scatter across the courtyard and out into the piazza. The plump, young German from Cologne quivers and convulses. He topples over, dead before he hits the stones.

2

Doug Gunther's bedroom is gloomy in the dawning. A jay squawks from a limb of the flowering cherry in the side yard. It darts up to scratch in the leafy gutter muck for grubs. Doug shifts and twitches beneath the bedclothes. Dreaming.

A car horn sounds a short, sharp blast down the block. The bureaucrats are already astir and rolling toward the Potomac.

He's in his classroom. A version of it anyway, but cleaner, brighter, infinitely more inviting. That's his writing on the blackboard, his briefcase on the table, his eviscerated toad on the tray by the soapstone sink.

His students sit at their usual desks, but they've been reworked as well. They're tidy, attentive, bright-eyed. Mr. Lomax, the halfback, has given over his usual tank top and backwards Braves cap for a dinner jacket and ascot.

Mr. Sykes, the chess geek, wears an impeccably pressed powder-blue dress shirt completely scoured of ink stains and pizza drippings. He looks to have even washed and combed his hair.

And then there's Amber. Beautiful Amber with her year-round tan, her blonde mane, her hazel eyes. She has elected to wear a crocheted thong to class and the diamond navel stud that Doug finds achingly distracting. What's more, no gum, no lavender nail polish. Just the serious, penetrating stare of a Fulbright scholar.

Doug flops onto his back with fluttering eyelids and smiles.

He leans against the lectern at the head of the classroom. He's briefly troubled to see that he has forgotten his shirt and wears his tie around his bare neck. But he's consoled to find he has remembered his trousers.

For his text, Doug consults a copy of Cosmopolitan magazine--all eye shadow and cleavage on the cover.

"Now," he says and gazes out over his flock of riveted, adoring students, "who can name the three orders of living amphibians?"

Hands shoot up. The students groan and plead.

"I know! I know! Please, Mr. Gunther! I know!"

Amber lifts her slender, nut-brown index finger. She trains on Doug the melting gaze that is God's gift to teen-aged girls.

"Amber," Doug says.

He motions for Amber to stand. She rises in her crocheted thong.

"They would be the apoda, the caudata, and the anura, Mr. Gunther."

"Precisely, Amber. Thank you"

Amber wriggles slowly back into her seat.

Doug consults the sexual dysfunction survey in his Cosmo.

"Who can name the country that borders Equatorial Guinea to the north?" he asks.

Hands shoot into the air.

"I know! I know!

The students wave their arms wildly, groan with the strain.

"Please, Mr. Gunther. Me! Me!"

Doug makes a show of glancing about the room as prelude to calling on Amber.

"Douglas," he hears. "I know."

The voice is low, brittle, adult. He looks for its source.

"Douglas," he hears again. "I know."

Doug lays his Cosmo aside on the lectern. He walks along a row of desks.

"Douglas," he hears. "Douglas"

She sits behind Mr. Lomax and is hidden at first by his bulk. She wears her paisley hospital gown. A drainage tube snakes out of her right nostril. An I.V. tube hangs from her arm. They lie loose and unconnected on the tile floor.

She is ashen. Frail. Ravaged.

11

"Douglas," she says in a raspy whisper, "I know."
"Gail?"
Slowly and with great effort, she rises to her feet. She is positively cadaverous, hideous to look upon. She struggles for breath.
"Cameroon," she says.

Doug jerks awake with a cry. An alarm chirps on his bedside table. Doug reaches blindly and slaps it into silence. He feels about the nightstand. Finding a framed photograph, he draws it to him. In the picture, they are posed before a rail fence. Jenny is seven and sits on the top rail between her mom and dad. Doug's arm is draped around his daughter and his wife.

Gail's smile is radiant. She is beautiful. Vibrant. Undiagnosed. Doug clutches the photo to his chest. He burrows with it beneath the bedclothes.

Doug steps from his bedroom into the hallway wearing his ratty, mismatched sweat suit -- half Georgetown, half U.V.A, but uniformly frayed and threadbare.

He is very nearly perspiring. He has scrupulously performed his twenty-five abdominal crunches. He has managed seventeen leg lifts of the twenty he intended. He has decided to save his push-ups for bedtime.

He eases open Jenny's bedroom door and switches on the overhead light.

"Let's go."

Jenny draws her blanket over her head and whines. "Ten more minutes."

"Six-forty. We're running late."

Doug can't imagine how she can bear the smell. He sniffs at the swampy air and glances about the room. Jenny's shelves and tabletops are crowded with terrariums and cages. They hold toads and garden snakes, turtles, salamanders, a bright green iguana -- Sally.

12

Her desk is stacked with field guides, herpetology texts, a National Geographic amphibian picture book, which she saved her own money to buy.

She has a photo of an orange and cobalt poison-dart frog taped to her dresser mirror. A framed print of Natasha Kinski --clothed only in a boa constrictor-- hangs over her bed.

Doug suspects Jenny is the only creature on the planet who bought the thing for the snake.

"Let's move it." He grabs a fistful of blanket and whips it off the bed.

Doug is two sections into the *Post* and halfway through his pot of coffee before Jenny shows up in the kitchen. She wears brogans, cargo pants, and a print blouse --a paramilitary mallrat.

She brings a foil packet of frosted Pop-Tarts to the table and spills them out onto a placemat.

"I need a note for the museum," Jenny says as she settles in to read the back of Doug's paper.

"A what?"

"The field trip, Daddy! I need a note so they'll let me out of school!"

"In a minute. Did you lay out my clothes?"

"Kind of." She picks at her Pop Tart. She pinches off bits of crust along the edges.

"Have you fed everybody?"

Jenny nods.

"Homer and Hal? Sally? Kermit?"

She nods.

"Lucifer?"

Jenny groans. She drags herself up from the table and crosses to the refrigerator. She fishes a hunk of lettuce from the crisper drawer.

Jenny huffs conspicuously as she stomps across the kitchen toward the laundry room door.

Lucifer, a jet-black guinea pig, hunkers in the cedar chips in his cage on the laundry table. As Jenny drops in the hunk of lettuce, she notices a chartreuse necktie on the floor alongside the dryer. Bright pink checks. Cobalt stripes. Something her father bought back when he used to be allowed to shop.

Jenny plucks it from the floor. She whisks it free of grit. Picks it clean of lint. "This'll do," she says.

3

Patrick Henry High School, home of the Fighting Marauders, is a sprawling Romanesque pile of a building. Doug Gunther climbs the stairs to the front landing where the key club boys and the drill team girls gather in the mornings to put themselves on display.

There is audible giggling as Doug passes. He eyes his socks. They look brown to him. As do his trousers. As does his jacket. As does his tie with the checks and the stripes.

Entering the building, Doug is jolted by his morning whiff of eau de high school--a heady blend of sour milk and gym clothes. As he heads toward the office to check his box, he sees Janice lingering in the hallway, reading a memo.

Black and sharp-tongued, she is Doug's best friend at school. Just about his only friend anywhere. Doug is almost upon her before she notices him. She shakes her head and smiles.

Janice takes Doug's tie in hand. She draws it out of his jacket.

"Bad?" Doug asks.

Janice loosens the knot. "What did you do to her?" She whips the tie off of Doug's neck.

Doug shrugs as Janice leads him along the hallway. Doug yawns and stretches. He tousles his hair, which was none too neat to begin with.

"I've got to tell you, Dougie, you look like hell."

"I've been having these really odd dreams. They wake me up."

"Odd how?"

15

"I'm running. I'm swimming. I'm falling off cliffs. I'm climbing trees. I'm milking goats. That kind of thing."

They draw abreast of a couple in the hallway. Students. The two lean together against a row of lockers in an embrace. They kiss moistly and adenoid deep.

Janice snaps her fingers. The crack is like a rifle shot. "Hey!"

The students unclench and slink off along the hallway.

"Milking goats?" she says.

Doug nods. "And then last night . . .Gail. I was teaching class, and she was there. It was really weird."

Doug swivels his head to stretch and work his neck. He reaches to knead his shoulder. "I'm all kinked up too. Maybe I'm just coming down with something."

Janice treats Doug to a fierce, flinty glare.

"You're not pulling this crap. You're not getting out of this."

"Out of what?"

Janice enters her empty classroom. Doug follows.

"Out of what?"

He earns a sidelong glance from Janice as she approaches her desk. She opens a drawer and produces a half dozen neckties in a clump--Doug's spares.

"Don't tell me you forgot. Barbara is very excited."

Janice selects a tie and holds it up to Doug's jacket. Satisfied, she turns up his collar and loops the tie around his neck.

"All kinked up," she snorts as she deftly forms a knot.

"That's not tonight is it?"

"You know damn well it is."

"Aw, Janice, You know I hate getting fixed up. I'm just not ready for . . ."

Janice jerks the knot snugly against Doug's neck with force enough to stun him.

"I don't want to hear it. Gail's been dead three years. It's time."

"But I've got papers to grade, and I'm way behind on all my . . ."

"Seven sharp. Kinks and all."

Janice fingers Doug's sports coat with a disapproving frown. "And wear something nice, will you?"

Wounded, Doug eyes his jacket. Brown. He retreats toward the classroom door, pausing by the jamb.

"Oh," he says, "what country borders Equatorial Guinea to the north?"

Janice pulls down a window shade map hanging over her blackboard. She slides her finger south along the Ivory Coast of Africa and finds her mark.

"Cameroon," she tells him.

Somehow he'd feared she would.

4

A clutch of tourists, their luggage at their feet, stands on the molo by the San Marco basin. They wait for the ferry to Marco Polo airport on the mainland.

Among them is a couple from Hagerstown, long married and worn raw with cramped hotel living and a solid week of each other's company. The husband, queasy and ill, has taken poorly to the food.

"An eel isn't a blessed thing but a snake in the water," his wife tells him. "Any fool knows that."

He burps as she digs through the smallest of the their half dozen suitcases. She reminds him, once again, that she would rather have gone to Paris.

She draws a pint-sized jar of antacid tablets from the suitcase. There is a flash of scarlet at her feet. A red lizard scurries up the shoulder strap of the small open suitcase and disappears inside.

A young man from London stands a few feet away snapping photographs. Yet another view of the delicate, pink, Moorish facade of the Palazzo Ducale. Again the Salute. He fishes his telephoto lens from the camera bag at his feet. Once more the Redentore across the water on the Giudecca.

A red lizard lingers between his feet, hidden in shadow. It darts to his camera bag and wriggles into a side pouch with his post cards and pilfered hotel stationery.

Another lizard darts to an iron mooring at the water's edge. It scurries along the underside of a braided hawser tethered to a motor launch, which has been lowered from the *Kirov* of Odessa.

Tourists tromp up and down the gracefully arched bridge adjacent to the Doge's Palace. They pose at the rail for photos, consult maps, clot headway.

A scarlet lizard scurries along the granite cap of the railing. It is conspicuous against the stone. Schoolgirls shriek. Grown men leap aside. The creature leaves an uproar in its wake as it descends to the embankment, darts left, and climbs the stucco facade of a chapel.

It moves quickly across the breadth of the building and around a corner into a Venetian side street.

Shadow consumes it but for the dim, malevolent glow of its yellow eyes as it pauses, clinging to the sidewall. With the sudden, unsettling rasp of claw on stone, it vanishes altogether.

5

Beatrice Malloy walks from her bus stop at D and Sixth due south to Constitution. She crosses the avenue and climbs the grand stairway of the National Gallery with the guards, the cloakroom girls, and the docents.

Beatrice is the sort of woman who would be unambiguously lovely if she would permit it, but she chooses to wear dully colored, frumpy clothes, which she thinks of as business-like and conservative. She tends toward flats to walk the gallery floor that look vaguely orthopedic. She often pulls and pins her hair back in a fashion that is severe and unflattering.

Nights at home with the hairpins out and the tweedy, untailored suit back in the closet, Beatrice is tempted to think herself exotic and maybe a little lovely. She is the product of an uncommon mix. Her mother is the daughter of a glass blower from Murano, in the outer Venetian lagoon. Her father is second generation Irish from Brookline, and the northern Italian/North Sea blend works stunningly for her those rare occasions when she allows it to.

Beatrice enters through the grand, front doorway. She glances sourly at Dali's Last Supper on display in the foyer and continues into the cavernous rotunda. She pauses to scan the space.

"Please, please, please, please," she chants lowly. It works. No Howard.

He thinks he loves her. He has taken to volunteering at the gallery to be near her. He is evermore inviting her to join him for coffee in the basement cafe.

Though hardly an ogre, Howard is relentless and a little pathetic. Somehow he has grown to adore her

20

veneer. Dowdy. Dull. Solid. The plain brown wrapper Beatrice shows to the world.

As is her custom at the top of the day, Beatrice visits the Italian gallery. The Venetians specifically. A particular Carpaccio on this morning. She keeps a wary eye for Howard, as she draws up before the canvas.

It is an interior, the upper floor of a palazzo. Dazzling Venetian sunlight washes in from a balcony illuminating an intricately woven rug. Beatrice leans close to study a dab of Carpaccio's trademark red in the pattern.

A hand touches her arm. She gasps and starts, turns with dread, fearing Howard. She sees instead Amy, her secretary who has her latest in a series of well-thumbed steno pads in hand.

"I hate to bother you, but Mr. Seville called."

"What now?"

"He's got a problem with our shipping procedures, and reservations about our transit insurance. He's threatening to pull both pieces out of the show."

"I'll talk him down. Anything else."

Amy consults her pad.

"A Katherine Simon from Random House. Some permission fee question. And Ted checked in. He's lobbying for lunch at Chan's."

Beatrice takes a last glance at the Carpaccio. She sets out with Amy across the gallery floor. "That boy's got a moo shu jones."

They approach a pair of women -- volunteers, smartly dressed, junior-league types who are admiring a Veronese. It is a massive depiction of the triumphant return of the Doge Marino Falieri to Venice following his defeat of the Dalmatians. It's little short of lurid with competing washes of color.

The brunette of the two, the one in espadrilles, turns to address Beatrice as she passes.

"Excuse us."

"Yes."

The woman gestures toward the painting. "Who did this?"

Beatrice points out the engraved brass wall plaque with the particulars etched on it.

"Paolo Veronese," she says, "1565. It's called the . . ."

The other one chimes in, the one with the frosted highlights and the Prada handbag.

"No, no. The frame."

"It's beautiful," the one in the espadrilles says. She and her friend admire the gilt work, the carving. They ignore the canvas altogether.

"Can't really say. That's kind of how it came."

The women smile and nod.

"Thanks so much, dear," the one with the highlights says and gives Beatrice a pat on the arm.

Beatrice responds with a rigid smile and continues with Amy across the gallery floor, muttering corrosively.

"Hi," she hears.

Beatrice stops and turns. She grins as sweetly as she can manage.

"Howard. What a pleasant surprise."

****

They are conspicuously unimproved. Doug knows it immediately as he enters his classroom to find Mr. Lomax, the halfback, scratching at a troublesome pustule under his tank top strap.

Doug checks Gail's seat. It's occupied by the sullen towheaded boy in the jean jacket who's name he can never remember. He draws pictures of cars in his binder throughout class every day. Only Fords. Usually Mustangs.

"Morning class."

As Doug approaches his desk, he glances toward Amber. Gum. Nail polish. Her boyfriend's fatigue jacket.

"I'm still short a few notes from home. If you want to go to the museum tomorrow, get 'em in."

"What if we don't want to go?"

It's Lomax. He's moved on to a wart on his wrist. He squeezes it mercilessly.

"You get to paint lockers with Mr. Jeffers." Assistant principal. Comb-over. Born again. Even the towheaded boy in the back groans. "Anybody else?"

Doug scans the room. He notices that Amber wears, under the fatigue jacket, a short knit top. It looks to him crocheted. She shifts in her seat. Doug catches the glint of her diamond navel stud. A corner of a magazine peeks out from beneath her stack of books. It looks vaguely like a Cosmo.

The spooky coincidences are piling up. Doug decides to take a flyer.

"Who can name the three orders of living amphibians?" he asks.

As one, the students avoid his gaze.

"Amber?"

She is so stricken and mortified that she stops chewing her gum.

"Mr. Gunther, I didn't read the . . ."

"That's okay."

Doug motions for her to stand. She rises unsteadily to her feet.

"The three orders of living amphibians. Give it a shot."

She rises nervously, silently. Amber can come up with nothing to say. She bursts into tears.

"I think I've got cramps!" she blubbers. She gathers her books and races out of the room.

"Hey, man, can guys get cramps?" It's Lomax. He's working on a hangnail with his incisors.

Doug draws his textbook from his briefcase and slaps it down on the lectern.

"No," he says. "Just coronaries."

23

****

Beatrice's office is a cluttered disaster. It's piled high with outdated paperwork, art books, museum catalogs, magazines. Beatrice settles in behind her desk with a cup of coffee. She hears her telephone ring, under something. She hears Amy's voice through the intercom, under something.

"It's your mom on two."

Beatrice digs through the paperwork, burrowing toward her handset. "Ciao, Mamma. Come va."

Beatrice's mother is bursting with the usual news. The miserable Boston spring weather. A new recipe for ground turkey. A cousin, freshly betrothed. Beatrice's father's prostate. Crime in the streets. The price of nectarines. That cretin in the White House. And did she mention Beatrice's cousin, freshly betrothed?

"Yeah, Mamma, I know. Clara is getting married. Some nice boy from Medford."

Ted sticks his head around the office door, but only so far as the bridge of his nose. He peeks in at Beatrice. She gestures vigorously for him to enter. He obliges, carrying a shopping bag.

Ted greets the clutter with a hand clapped to his mouth-- his preference in stagy, horrified expressions. He uncovers a chair, shifting a half dozen back issues of *Il Gazzettino* onto the floor, and sits.

He perches with his legs crossed, his shopping bag beside him on the rug. He smiles primly at Beatrice. Ted is radioactively gay. Catty, snide, dramatic, sentimental, fit, witty, elegantly beautiful.

He has been in a committed relationship for the past seven years with a deputy undersecretary of state named Duane. Ted and Duane share a taste in light opera and little else. They bicker constantly, periodically leave each other for good, and reconcile over weekend shopping binges.

"I've got to go, Mom. Ted's here. No, still gay."

Ted makes a show of bitchy indignation.

"I'll tell him." Ciao." Beatrice cradles the receiver. "Mom says butch up."

"As if!"

Ted plucks up his shopping bag. He carries it to Beatrice's desk.

"Duane and I came across the most glorious tag sale in Warrenton. I thought of you."

Ted pulls from the bag a green pillbox hat with a half veil and a pair of white kid gloves, elbow-length. He sets them before Beatrice.

"If you're going to do this Mamie Eisenhower thing,"--Ted gestures to take in Beatrice's ensemble--"go the whole hog, sugar."

Beatrice fingers the gloves, the hat. "You're a wicked man."

The veil is attached to the hat with a long pin that Beatrice extracts with menacing deliberation. She smiles at Ted. He knows her well enough to run.

6

An Al Italia 747 lifts off from Da Vinci International east of Rome. It vectors north, gains altitude over the Tyrrhenian Sea, and levels out at thirty-five thousand feet.

In the belly of the fuselage, baggage containers jostle and creak with the movement of the plane. The compartment is dark, nearly pitch black. A bit of light seeps around a lower galley bulkhead door with an imperfect seal. A prick of it escapes through a vacant screw hole in the floor of the passenger cabin above.

Atop a far container at the aft end of the compartment, the yellow eyes of a lizard glow.

The craft banks gracefully, due east at forty degrees, Dulles bound.

****

The Kirov of Odessa, a rusting pleasure liner, drops its moorings and eases out of its slip at the Stazione Marittima in the Venetian harbor.

The passengers wave, shout, and shoot streamers from the railings as the massive ship steams between the Zattere and the Giudecca. It swings briefly north between the ancient customs house and San Giorgio Maggiore, bringing the Piazza San Marco into view.

Late afternoon sunlight illuminates the southern facade of the Doge's Palace. Tourists swarm along the molo. Gondolas bob on the chop like debris.

Finding the channel, the Kirov comes about to an easterly bearing and steams clear of the Lido, into the open Adriatic.

The ship is dowdy topside and positively squalid beneath the waterline. The lower holds are heaped with spare parts and hardware. They're soggy with oil-fouled ballast. Overrun with rats.

The creatures are plump, slow-footed, insolent. One particularly meaty specimen sprawls on its side upon fifty-pound sack of rice. It twitches and jiggles oddly.

A scarlet lizard lifts its head from its meal of the rat's soft belly. Its snout is bloody, dripping with giblets. It glances fiercely about, its jaundiced eyes aglow.

7

Beatrice Malloy jogs through Georgetown, east along Dumbarton. She wears baggy, gray sweats and ratty, canvas sneakers. The left one is held together with duct tape.

Her apartment key, placed for safekeeping in her sock, has slid awkwardly into her shoe. With each stride, it gouges a bit of skin from her instep. She intends to perch on the curb and draw it out, but at every corner she meets with more joggers and keeps running -- prodded to compete.

Three women, sheathed in Lycra, run her down with ease and zip past her. They chat with each other and laugh. They are not in respiratory agony like she is. A man races past pushing a three-wheeled baby stroller.

Beatrice stops with a groan. "Fuck it!" She plops down on the sidewalk and jerks off her shoe.

Beatrice swings by a newsstand on Wisconsin. She walks there. Tony, the proprietor, special orders Italian newspapers for her. *La Republica. Il Gazzettino.* She picks them up every weeknight, carries them home, and neglects to read them.

She used to hope --in an idle and dreamy sort of way-- that she would wander in one night to pick up her papers and meet a man. He would approach her at the register. He would greet her in Italian. He would carry a dog-eared copy of Petrarch in his pocket.

But then she'd actually met one.

"Buona sera," he'd told her.

It proved to be the full extent of his Italian. His name was Robert, but his friends called him Bruno. Annuities were his livelihood. Racquetball his passion.

28

The Redskins his religion. Now she just hopes she's not robbed on the way home.

She lives in a gracelessly dilapidating 30th Street townhouse on what would have been the parlor floor. Her apartment rivals her office in clutter. She has accepted that she is not tidy. She is at peace with her slovenliness except when the occasional stack of books topples over and endangers Gus, her cat.

She only cleans in spasms --when her parents visit, when she entertains a date. The magazines have piled up. She has a month's worth of *Posts* heaped in a corner. The Tintoretto print she's been meaning to hang still leans against the wall by the TV. She's not had callers in a while.

Beatrice sits on the sofa with Gus purring in her lap. With one hand, she scratches his head. With the other she manipulates the television remote, rifling through the channels. She forages, lights briefly, and moves on -- like a man.

She is approaching cable Siberia at the upper end of the dial -- Fox News, HGTV, The Country Music Channel-- when she comes across a talking head on C-Span. It is the senior senator from Kentucky, Royce Tillman. He is notorious, even by D.C. standards, for his sweeping banalities.

Tillman is a search-and-destroy conservative with an unpersuasive salt and pepper toupee. He specializes in ridicule and venom. He has made a thriving congressional career out of belittling immigrants. Women. Bleeding hearts. And Godless sodomites (he calls them).

He claims to stand for the solid American principles of our founding fathers. He will often weep openly in the presence of the flag. He once recalled receiving a wound in a battle in Hue City until he learned that he'd been in Alabama instead. In the Washington manner, by way of apology, he simply forgot that he'd recalled it.

His wife of twenty-seven years, Delores, serves him in a professional capacity as his wife of twenty-seven years, Delores. She is capable of gazing lovingly upon him and, when need be, pecking him chastely upon the lips. She is blonde. Thin. Brittle. Desperate to be forty again.

As a rule, Beatrice Malloy is thoroughly indifferent to politics, but Senator Tillman is a special case. He is powerful and respected. He controls countless funding streams--the National Gallery's among them. He is also the local gold standard for mendacity. Beatrice can't help but linger over the sight of him.

"I think there's no question the E.P.A.'s reaction is politically motivated, which I find deeply, deeply troubling."

The beady eyes. The laughable rug. The Cosa Nostra manicure. The unrelieved hypocrisy.

"We're talking spit in the ocean. Biochem has generously funded the cleanup. No fish kills in over a month. And the water tests nearly pure. I think these simpering, knee-jerk tree-huggers have got their bandanas tied too tight."

Gus leaps to the floor. He wheezes twice and deposits a hairball onto the rug.

Beatrice stands to fetch the ammonia. She switches off the set and tosses the remote aside.

"Amen," she tells him.

8

Jenny eats spaghetti in the kitchen. The microwave variety. It is incendiary at the outer edges and frosty at the core. Welded with cheese into an unappetizing lump, it clatters and rattles on her plate.

Mrs. Wrenn sits across the table from Jenny with her nose in a *Guidepost*. Jenny didn't want a sitter. She especially didn't want Mrs. Wrenn, who watches the television at full volume and makes Jenny kiss her good night. A mouthful of face powder. A snoutful of perfume.

Jenny lays her cheek on her palm and pokes at her semi-frozen spaghetti with her fork.

This is how Doug finds her. Sullen. Irritated. He immediately checks his clothes. Brown, top to bottom. He charges Mrs. Wrenn to tell him how he looks.

"Very nice," she says.

"You look swell, Daddy."

That's what Jenny always says.

"Help me out here. I'm going for neat but uninterested."

Jenny directs him to turn around. She looks him up and down.

"What's her name?"

"Barbara. She's some kind of banker."

"Show her your checkbook. That ought to do it."

Janice and Hank live but a couple of miles away, just inside of the Leesburg Pike. Doug has turned onto their block and is in sight of their house before he has manufactured the first scrap of serviceable patter. He draws to the curb and stops.

In the unlikely event that Barbara is a suitable match, Doug will need a handful of sterling remarks. He has lately grown persuaded that he has no spontaneous, natural charm to fall back on. In the event that Barbara is colossally wrong for him -- a near certainty-- he will want to be transparently dull, a living narcotic.

Sitting at the curb in his Camry, painfully obvious and irrelevant observations come to him in waves. Here in the shank of his third decade, Doug seems to have grown into a gift for tediousness.

He can hear Barbara talking from the porch. He means to ring the bell. He even lays his finger to it, but he hesitates.

"To tell you the truth, I didn't have the first clue what to do with it. I didn't know if you boiled it, or you peeled it, or you fried it. I just didn't know. I mean who ever heard of a tomatillo when I was a little girl."

Doug decides he will feel poorly just after dinner and just before dessert. He will be feverish. He will need to go straight home.

"The produce man straightened me out, and they were just delicious. A little lemony, a little tomatoey. Who knew!?"

Doug actively entertains the thought of creeping off the porch and driving home. He is wondering what sort of evil, violent things Janice would do to him as Hank swings open the door for some air.

"Doug!"

"Hammerin' Hank."

Doug lingers on the porch. He makes no move toward the doorway. Hank speaks to Doug lowly, through the doorscreen.

"Take me with you."

"Come on in, boys."

It's Janice. She has risen from the settee to join Hank at the door. She lays her hand to Hank's back in that fashion that looks, to the untrained eye, loving and tender. She pinches him. He manages an agonized smile and shoves open the door screen.

"Get yourself in here, buddy."

Barbara is a lovely brunette. She's tall, willowy, impeccably fit. She runs nights, through Georgetown, in Lycra. She is a loan officer and earns, unlike Doug, a living wage. She owns her apartment. She is wholly unattached. She has been, she claims, too busy for men.

As Doug sits listening to her, a benign smile on his lips, he suspects that she could do justice to a diamond navel stud and a crocheted thong. As Doug sits listening to her, he pictures her in glamorous eveningwear--pearls, heels, a sheer off-the-shoulder gown. As Doug sits listening to her, he envisions her in the pearls alone. As Doug sits listening to her, he realizes that she is constitutionally incapable of shutting up.

He can't breathe. His brain has gone numb. His eyes won't focus. He fears getting nattered to death.

Barbara has recently read a novel about a man who can communicate telepathically with dogs. She describes it in exhaustive detail. She has watched, in the past week, an interview on television with an actress she greatly admires. Barbara has purchased, at that actress's suggestion, the collected works of L. Ron Hubbard.

Scientology somehow leads Barbara back to tomatilloes which remind her of jicama and its delightful crunch in salads.

So far, Doug has only said, "Yes, thanks," when Hank offered him a beer.

Over dinner, Barbara occasionally interrupts herself to giggle and say, "I talk too much." Then she continues.

When Janice rises to clear the dishes, Doug leaps to his feet. He plucks up a couple of saucers and beats her to the kitchen.

"Good Lord, Janice!"

"She's just nervous."

Janice pours a carafe of water into her drip coffee machine. She switches it on. It sputters and gurgles.

Hank pushes open the swinging door a crack and sticks his head into the kitchen like a drowning man coming up for air. "Doug," he pleads.

Barbara is still talking. Her childhood in Atlanta. Her sorority at Sweetbriar. Her personal fascination with Enya.

"Get back in there!" Janice snaps.

Hank grimly withdraws from sight.

Doug watches Janice set a tray on the counter. He sees her freight it with cups and saucers. A cream pitcher. A sugar dish.

"If you try to give that woman caffeine, I'll have to kill you."

Doug finds Mrs. Wrenn asleep before the television, her *Guidepost* open upon her lap. He switches off the set and awakens Mrs. Wrenn with a nudge. He pays her and escorts her to her car in the drive.

She demands, as is her custom, that he kiss her on the cheek. Face powder. Perfume.

Doug slowly makes his way upstairs, turning off lights, trying doors. He makes his way in the dark along the hallway to his bedroom where he undresses by the light of the bare bulb in the closet, which hangs thick with clothes. Relatively few of them are his. Most are Gail's.

He knows he should have long since gotten rid of them. Janice has, more than once, provided him with a number to call. They'll send a truck to pick them up and haul them off.

Doug decides, again, to dial it tomorrow. He hangs up his jacket. He draws out between his fingers the gauzy sleeve of one of Gail's print dresses. Brown. He presses it to his face.

Faintly, thinly, her scent still clings.

2

On the Ruga Giuffa, an ancient Venetian calle, a scarlet lizard scuttles along a scaling stucco sidewall. It moves just above the doorways of the shops and the wine bars, darting with alarming velocity toward a patch of sunlight. Toward an elegantly arched bridge which rises over a canal and gives onto the Campo Di Santa Maria Formosa.

The square is wide, bright, airy. A husband and wife--Texans-- reconnoiter in the bright Adriatic sun. They study a map, seeking a route to the Accademia Bridge.

The wife senses movement on the underside of the bridge railing.

"Look at that pretty bug."

She approaches and bends for a better view. It's not a bug after all. A lizard, implausibly red. She's never seen a red lizard, even in Texas.

The creature's gullet distends. Its jaws hinge open. It hisses. The noise is sudden and joltingly loud. Like steam from a pipe. She dances away from the railing with a shriek.

On the far side of the campo, a door swings open, and an odd little hook-nosed man emerges from his house. He is slight and white-haired. He is stooped and fairly consumed by his cavernous serge blazer.

He wanders across the campo toward the canopied vegetable stand in the shaded westerly quarter of the square.

He admires the meaty artichoke hearts floating in a tub, the bitter greens, the plump tomatoes. The blood oranges are in full season and irresistible. He requests

35

two kilos and then turns quickly about. He squints toward the arched bridge.

He hears his name.

He must go.

As in a dream, the odd little man strays from the fruit stand. He walks slowly but resolutely toward the bridge across the campo.

The produce vendor, weighing out oranges on his scale, calls after him. "Signore. Signore!"

He hears his name.

He must go.

The couple from Texas watches him approach. His stare is glassy, fixed. He walks with sluggish deliberation, laboriously placing one foot in front of the other.

They look on as he gains the bridge railing. He extends his open hand toward the scarlet lizard. The wife claps her hands to her ears, but the creature crawls onto his palm without a sound.

He covers it gently. He lifts his hands to his face as if in prayer.

A wisp of brilliant, scarlet smoke escapes from between his fingers, followed by another, and another, until bright, red smoke is boiling and seething from between his hands. He inhales deeply. Scarlet smoke courses in through his nostrils. A thick cloud of it drifts skyward.

"Jesus, Stanley, take a picture!"

This is just the sort of thing they'll simply never believe in Lubbock.

The odd little man parts his hands. Red ash drops to the cobbles. Is lost to the breeze.

He must go.

He turns and walks, moving slowly, steadily across the campo. He swings open the weathered door of his modest house. He draws it firmly shut behind him.

The tarnished brass plate affixed to the sun-bleached door rail is engraved with the name 'Matteo Falieri'.

36

10

Senator Royce Tillman lavishes unseemly notice upon the posterior of a congressional page. Illuminated by a shaft of sunlight, her skirt has become transparent. She is shapely and long in the inseam. Stirringly long, Senator Tillman decides.

"She's stringing for the New York Times."

"I'm sorry, what?"

Senator Tillman brushes lint from his jacket. He adjusts the lay of his erection.

Jack Proctor starts again, from the top.

"This is Lewis." He indicates a young man to his right. Lewis wears a navy sports coat and khakis, last year's power tie. He is from Lexington. He will attend U.K. in the fall. He is barely nineteen and has a passion for civics. He has waited three years to be selected an intern.

"Lewis'll go with you to the Mall for the shoot. The photographer's name is Lisa Dodd. She's stringing for the *Times*. I've told her she has half an hour. We've got Reverend Cleveland at one."

"Lisa Dodd. Right. The good reverend at one."

Senator Tillman pats the cowlick of his unpersuasive hairpiece with his palm. A nervous tic.

"Who is that?" he asks and points to the leggy page. Casually, he thinks.

"I don't know, sir."

Jack Proctor wears an elegantly tailored gray suit. An eagle lapel pin. This year's power tie. He is gaunt, severe-- all veiny sinew and bone.

"Find out."

Proctor produces a notepad. He makes a show of jotting a reminder. But he has already found out. Her

37

name is Melanie. She is the daughter of a self-made soda-bottling magnate and dewy-eyed patriot from Connecticut.

Proctor has it on good authority that she has bedded a member of the Michigan congressional contingent and was interrupted in a lavatory while performing an intimate service upon the press secretary of the minority whip.

Proctor intends to prevent her from graduating to the senate. He has called in a favor. She will be reassigned to the Library of Congress. Today.

"Yes sir. I'll get right on it."

Proctor folds shut his notebook. He slips it back into his pocket.

"All right, Larry. It's me and you," Senator Tillman says and strikes out down the corridor.

"It's Lewis, sir." Lewis hustles to catch up.

Tillman slaps him fondly on the back.

"Of course it is."

Doug is mildly queasy from the jostling and the exhaust. He rides beside Jenny on the seat just behind the driver, Mrs. Stone. She is out of practice with buses. She no longer works a regular route.

She is a substitute for Mr. Gaither who is home with the flu. Mrs. Stone teaches girl's gym and something called "Health" -- a scholastic blend of *Penthouse* Forum and study hall.

She drives with a lead foot, weaving in and out of traffic on Interstate 66. A man in a Volvo cuts her off on the ramp to the Roosevelt Bridge, and she calls him -- quite loudly -- a cocksucker.

Mr. Lomax is, once again, tormenting Mr. Sykes in the back of the bus. Doug can hear the pitiful whimpering, the occasional sharp cries of pain. But his stomach is unsettled, and he hardly feels fit to lurch once more down the aisle.

Mrs. Stone spares him the touble. She addresses Mr. Lomax in her rearview mirror with a scalding dose of profanity. She informs him she will stop the bus. She assures him she will snatch him bald.

She swings onto Constitution Avenue, pumping the brakes and blowing the horn. It is a beautiful spring day. The Mall is alive with tourists and idle bureaucrats taking the sun. The bus races past the Ellipse and the White House. It comes to a violent stop at the curb before the Museum of Natural History.

"There now," Mrs. Stone says and shoves open the doors.

They straggle, the students do. They are enormously deft at straggling. Even on the short walk from the bus to the Natural History Museum, they manage to splay out and drag. Doug is obliged to circle back and herd them along, drive them.

Jenny is the worst of the lot. When she begged to be allowed to come, she promised to be mindful and good. But she has removed her book bag and taken from it the pickle jar she plans to fill with bugs. Mall bugs for her iguana and her toads.

Jenny has decided they are weary of the local, suburban fare. She intends to surprise them with District bugs, meaty and exotic.

"Didn't we have a deal!?" Doug is yelling already. He hadn't meant to yell.

Jenny crawls through the grass, heading off a beetle. "I'm coming," she says.

Doug watches her. She's not coming.

"Hey!"

Four men on the sidewalk in their shirtsleeves, Justice Department types, turn around.

"I'm coming!" She stands and shoves her jar into her backpack. "Chill out, Dougie!"

Doug endures a brief and blinding temptation to sell her into slavery. He smiles sheepishly toward the men on the sidewalk. Three of them glare at him. The one with kids smiles back.

Once inside the museum, Doug's students are manageable. They behave just as they do in class. They are sluggish, barren of curiosity, and thoroughly inattentive. They brighten a bit in the presence of the dinosaurs, but their interest flags quickly. These are just bones. They've seen live ones at the movies.

Jenny walks with the class. Mr. Sykes, prince of the geeks, tries to chat her up, amuse her with a crack. But he is hopeless with females, even ten-year-olds.

Doug gathers them around a display of fossilized remains.

"Ichthyostega," he says, "the earliest known tetrapod. Notice how the skull flattens and tapers, almost into horns."

Only Jenny shows any interest. Doug's students peer dully, perfunctorily at the display.

The question is long overdue. He's been expecting it. He was counting on Mr. Lomax or perhaps Miss Brady, the Pep Club treasurer. Instead, the hand that goes up belongs to the towheaded boy in the denim jacket, the one who draws Fords.

Doug is stunned. The boy has been scrupulously quiet for the whole semester. This is a breakthrough.

"Yes?" Doug says eagerly and yields the floor.

"Are we going to have to know this?"

Mr. Seville is still unhappy. Beatrice is on her second call to him of the day. She talked to him three times yesterday. He refuses to be mollified. He vigorously confounds all of Beatrice's efforts to please him. Mr. Seville seems to prefer unhappiness.

He is the curator of a small, municipal museum in Ohio. Some months back, he agreed to lend the National Gallery a pair of Guarientos for a show. They are early, insignificant works. Smallish canvases. Heavily varnished. Murky.

Beatrice doesn't actually need them anymore. The show is complete without them. But now Mr. Seville is unhappy. He objects to their shipping procedures. He thinks their transit insurance wanting. He has grown surly and imperious. He speaks of his small, Ohio museum as if it were the Tate or the Louvre.

Beatrice feels duty bound to calm and to defuse him. She flatters his institution. She rhapsodizes over his taste. She becomes, immediately, wiser in his estimation.

"I feel that we are . . . simpatico," he tells her.

She readily agrees.

He confides that his wife doesn't understand him, that she fails to appreciate his virtues. He declares that they are emotionally estranged.

"I'm so sorry." Beatrice says it tenderly, sweetly.

"You know, I'm coming to D.C.," he declares. Perhaps drinks. Perhaps dinner. Perhaps . . .more.

Beatrice stifles a groan. She tells Mr. Seville that her desk has caught fire. She tells him she must go.

Ted taps on Beatrice's office door as he pushes it open before him. He finds Beatrice facedown on her blotter.

"Did you get Seville straightened out?"

"Oh yeah."

"Up for moo shu?"

Beatrice rises from her desk. She crosses to the door. She takes Ted by the hand.

"Come on. I'm going to broaden your horizons."

11

A family of four from Kentucky --from tiny
Maysville up by the border-- has waylaid their senior
senator on the D.C. Mall. Both husband and wife are
enthusiastic supporters.

"Come all the way up here and run into you. I'll just
be damned to hell."

The couple howls with laughter. Tillman chuckles
politely. He pats his toupee with his palm.

"I'd best be back about the nation's business," he
says and offers his hand.

The husband shakes it firmly. Tillman lifts the wife's
knuckles to his lips. Kisses them. Something to tell the
biddies back in Maysville.

"God bless you," she manages, choked with
emotion.

Lisa Dodd waits impatiently farther west along the
Mall, near Seventh Street. Royce Tillman has selected
her for study even before he notices the pair of battered
Nikons hanging around her neck.

She is tall, with a model's lankiness, and yet still
chesty(Tillman observes). She wears boots --lugged
soled, East Village. A short skirt. A man's sleeveless
undershirt beneath her weathered, leather jacket. No
make up. No bra.

"Here he comes."

It's Lisa Dodd's assistant, Tony. He removes a cloth
reflector from its nylon cover. Lisa Dodd takes a final,
vicious drag on her cigarette and flicks it away.

Tillman is even smarmier than she expected. His
toupee, more laughable. He kisses the back of her hand.
He apologizes for the delay.

"I've been hard at the nation's business," he informs her chest.

Tillman gestures vaguely toward Lewis, introduces him.

"Larry," he says.

Lisa Dodd intends to pose the senator with the Capitol over his shoulder. She blocks him through her viewfinder. She instructs him to shift and turn. He responds poorly, and she is obliged to situate him herself.

She grips him at the shoulders and ratchets him about. He brushes his crotch against her.

"I do beg your pardon," he tells her in an arch whisper.

Lisa Dodd tests for an exposure. She focuses. She takes a shot and brackets for two more. The senator admires her breasts.

"Eyes here, Senator." She points to the camera lens.

"Why of course, sugar."

She wants it. He can tell. He can always tell.

Tillman's gaze briefly comes to rest upon a woman. She stands behind Lisa Dodd, looking on. Doubtless, she finds him enchanting. Magnetic. What with his fame. His power. His hair replacement system.

He's convinced she would be lovely with a better cut of clothes. Heels, perhaps. A new coif. She continues to stare, helpless against his allure.

Beatrice Malloy takes a bite of her hotdog.

"Jesus," she says, chewing, "who'd want a picture of him?"

Ted nibbles at his bun. He finds the smell of the chili and the glistening grease on the wiener unsavory. He didn't care for the look of the cart, the hygiene of the vendor. He wanted moo shu.

"I think he likes you," Ted says.

"My luck."

Tillman glances toward Lisa Dodd. She bends revealingly. He can see down her shirt. He adjusts the lay of his erection.

"Hey!" The leggy photographer raises one of her Nikons high above her head. She points to the lens of it. "Eyes here!" she barks.

They sit on a grassy slope near the skating rink, just down from the Natural History Museum. They eat bagged lunches, prepared in the cafeteria. Pimento cheese. Corn chips. Sugar cookies. Gritty, powdered lemonade.

Mr. Lomax force feeds Mr. Sykes a clump of fescue. The towheaded boy in the denim jacket draws a Mustang on his napkin. Miss Brady, of the Pep Club, misidentifies buildings along the Mall. She points them out for Mr. Kruk, their Estonian exchange student.

"That one's the Freer." It's the Hirshhorn.

"That's the National Gallery." It's the Air and Space Museum.

"And that's the Smithsonian." It's the National Gallery.

Doug turns to see that Amber has shed her jacket and is stretched out upon it on the grass. She has pulled her blouse up to her bra line. She has unfastened her jeans. She is working on her tan. Her diamond navel stud sparkles in the sunlight.

Jenny collects bugs by the skating rink. She has dozens already -- spiders, beetles, crickets, a few sluggish flies. They are thick in the grass and easy to come by. She spies a beefy, black ant, and, as she crawls to corral it, she sees movement at the lip of the rink were the copper coping meets the cement. Devilishly quick. Scarlet.

Lewis taps his watch face. "Sir, we really need to get back."

"Just hold your water, son."

Tillman has removed his jacket. He's hooked his finger under the collar of it and poses in profile with the coat draped cavalierly over his shoulder, his free hand to his hip.

The shot is his idea. Hard-working. Blue collar. Man of the people.

Lisa Dodd draws him into focus. She takes a half dozen shots. They'll never use any of them in the *Times*, but she'll definitely want a few for her Christmas cards.

She composes the copy in her head:

Warmest Holiday Greetings
from
Senator Royce Tillman
Forthright. Committed. Aroused.

As Royce Tillman lifts his head and grinds his molars to conceal his jowly tendencies, he hears his name.

Lisa Dodd ratchets back an f-stop. Refocuses.

"Eyes here, Senator."

He must go.

He drops his jacket to the grass. He strays from Lisa Dodd's viewfinder. She lowers her camera.

"Senator?"

He hears his name.

He must go.

"If we're finished, you just have to say so." Lisa Dodd turns toward Lewis, fiery-eyed.

"What the hell's with him!?

Lewis shrugs. He tries on her the boyish smirk that the girls back in Lexington find winning.

Lisa Dodd slips her Nikons from around her neck. She flings them to Tony.

45

Beatrice and Ted look on as Senator Royce Tillman approaches Seventh Street, which dissects the Mall. He walks slowly. He fairly creeps along, setting one foot carefully in front of the other. His expression is slack, blank. His gaze is glassy.

Tillman steps into the roadway, heedless of traffic. A sedan swerves to avoid him. Its horn sounds. Tillman is oblivious, devoted only to his slow steady progress along the Mall.

"Senator!" It's Lewis, at a trot. "Senator Tillman!"

He jogs past Ted and Beatrice. He negotiates a gap in traffic and quickly catches up to Tillman as the senator veers right, toward the skating rink.

Lewis speaks to Tillman. Lewis pleads with Tillman. He circles the senator like a puppy--fretful, yapping, ignored.

Beatrice and Ted exchange identical glances. Slight smiles. Eyebrows lifted. They follow.

Doug collects the trash his students have left behind. He's sent them ahead with Mrs. Stone. He peers about for Jenny. Doug finds her on all fours by the skating rink, easing toward the railing.

"Jenny!"

"I'm coming."

He watches her. She's not coming.

Jenny has found it clinging to a baluster just above the coping. It is like nothing she has ever seen, not even in her books.

A skink, but such a color! Pure, brilliant red. Without variation. Without flaw. And the eyes!

Carefully and ever so slowly, Jenny reaches and traps the creature with her jar. It flicks its tongue. Its gullet distends. Its jaws hinge open. It hisses.

Tillman stops. Lewis clutches his elbow.

"Sir?"

Ted and Beatrice pause as well. Ted looks toward the rink by Constitution. "What in the world was that?"

Jenny giggles. She is fearless, delighted and quickly tightens down the lid.

She unzips her book bag and shoves the jar inside as the red skink spits a milky stream onto the glass. The bugs Jenny has collected -- the spiders and beetles, the crickets and ants and flies -- shrivel as if scorched and scalded. They drop dead to the jar bottom.

Lewis tugs at the senator's elbow. He can't budge him.

"We're running late, sir. Remember? One o'clock? The preacher?"

Senator Royce Tillman says lowly, "No!"

Doug tosses a fistful of napkins into a trash barrel. Jenny lingers still by the rink, fumbling with her book bag.

"Jenny!"

"I'm coming!"

He watches her. She is coming.

She promised her father, after Lucifer, no more pets. She promised him again after Sally, her iguana. She decides to wait a day or two before she undertakes to promise him again.

She works her arms through her book bag straps and runs toward the bus.

"Sir?" It's hopeless. Tillman won't budge. He watches a child running across the Mall toward Constitution.

"No!" Tillman is yelling now. Shrill. Anguished. "Piccina, vieni qua!"

Beatrice looks toward Ted, her mouth agape. It is Italian. Impeccably spoken. Native.

Jenny charges past Doug and boards the bus. Doug drops the last of the trash into a barrel by the walk as Tillman begins to wail.

"Piccina, vieni qua! E` mio! E` mio!"

47

Doug sees him drop to his knees. Tillman pitches about violently in the grass. Lewis kneels beside him, helpless to calm him. Beatrice and Ted stand watching.

Doug approaches to see if he can be of any assistance. He knows the Heimlich maneuver. He is familiar with cardiovascular pressure points. He is skilled in C.P.R..

Tillman flails about. Screaming.

"Eccolo! Eccolo! Mia lucertola! Mio condottiero!"

"What's he saying?" Ted asks Beatrice.

"There goes his lizard? His guide?"

She follows Tillman's dire glances toward a yellow school bus by the curb on Constitution. The Fighting Marauders.

Senator Royce Tillman weeps and wails. He thrashes wildly in the grass. His hair replacement system is ejected from his scalp.

"Senator. Senator."

Lewis shakes Tillman by the shoulders as a uniformed D.C. cop jogs toward them across the mall.

Doug nods a greeting to Ted and Beatrice.

"Is there anything I can do?"

"Ho 'un incarico!" Tillman shrieks.

"I doubt it."

The policeman arrives speaking into his radio. He is calling for an ambulance. He takes charge, shifting the gathering crowd back.

"Well," Doug says. He smiles at Beatrice. He turns and crosses toward the bus, which chugs away from the curb in a puff of blue smoke.

"Piccina!" Tillman is shrieking now. "Viene qua!"

"What's he saying?" Ted asks.

Beatrice watches Tillman watch the bus. It rounds the corner on Seventh toward Pennsylvania and rolls out of sight.

"Little girl," she says. "Come back."

12

Matteo Falieri, still wearing his oversized serge
blazer, stalks through his modest house on the Campo
Di Santa Maria Formosa.

He jerks open a cupboard drawer at the head of his
brief back hallway. He flings out the contents and sorts
through them on the floor. He selects an ornate silver
letter opener, one of his late wife's nail files.

He must go.

In the dining room, upon the heirloom mahogany
table, his bladed cutlery has been collected in a heap.
Butter knives. Jack knives. Steak knives. Poultry shears.
Paring knives. Boning knives. Cuticle scissors. Butcher
knives. A brace of Spanish cavalry sabers from over the
mantelpiece.

He adds the letter opener, and the nail file to the
heap. He busies himself --tidying, organizing, displaying.
Detached, efficient, he lays the cutlery out on the table in
neat rows. He works quickly, without pause or
reflection.

He must go.

Matteo Falieri considers his wares. He is deliberate,
thorough. His eyes move up one row of cutlery, down
the next. No piece is slighted, each weighed in turn.

He makes his selection with unswerving, clinical
resolve. He reaches for a knife. He eyes it blankly, the
hilt of it resting upon his palm. It is a fillet knife-- thin,
French. It is beautifully balanced. It is mercilessly sharp.

He applies the blade to the fleshy tip of his left
thumb, testing the edge with a quick, firm stroke. He
reaches bone.

He must go.

49

Matteo Falieri emerges from the chill shadows of the Calle degli Albanesi onto the bright, airy Riva alongside the lagoon. He turns east, toward the public gardens.

Two Australians, gloriously drunk, tumble out of the Hotel Danielli with the help of the concierge and three porters. A young man with a disposable, pasteboard camera stands at the edge of the embankment. He snaps pictures of the lagoon.

He sees an odd little man approaching along the Riva. The gentleman is vaguely hatchet-faced in the Venetian way--sharp, bony features, a prominent, angular nose. He is bleeding freely.

His left trouser leg is blood-soaked. His thumb is deeply gashed. He drips onto the stones. Oddly, he carries a kitchen knife in his good hand.

Falieri crosses the wide canal that passes before the Arsenale. He approaches the working-class district of Castello. As in all of Venice, the buildings here are dowdy and tumble-down. But not quaintly so. Without charm.

Falieri leaves the Riva for the Rio Terra Garibaldi-- formerly a waterway and now a cobbled street. He passes the iron gates of Garibaldi Park, which is overrun with cats. A woman in a housecoat feeds them scraps from her table. They swarm at her feet, Castello's answer to the pigeons of Piazza San Marco.

Falieri stops suddenly. He turns. Across the way, before a storefront, a young man unloads merchandise from a cart. Milk. Eggs. Tinned tomatoes.

As he wrestles with a sack of semolina, he hears a voice.

"Ah, signore."

An odd little man stands just before him. He is dapper, this odd little man. He is bloody. He smiles.

"ConoscoLei?" the young man asks. Do I know you?

Falieri steps closer still. "Per i suoi delitti," he says. For your crimes.

Efficiently, precisely, Matteo Falieri raises his knife and pricks the young man exactly twice. Two quick jabs to the base of his neck, one to either side, and his carotid arteries are cleanly severed.

The pain is brief. Surprising. Blood spurts from the punctures. The young man grows giddy and lightheaded. He decides he will sit. They are screaming already in the street.

Matteo Falieri finds the gap he is seeking, there between his ribs, just beside his sternum. The blade enters easily -- through flesh, through muscle, through ventricle wall. He smiles as he collapses.

Women wail. Men shout and charge along the cobbles. The old crone with the table scraps runs from the park, trailing cats.

A butcher cradles the young man in his arms, his apron glistening with blood. A crowd collects. Friends. Neighbors. Strangers. At their feet, cats circulate with sinewy grace --tabbys and manxes, brindles and blues. The bony orphans of Venice.

13

In the reception area of Senator Royce Tillman's office suite in the Dirksen Building, Jack Proctor offers the Reverend Mr. Cleveland more coffee.

"Just a splash, thank you."

Proctor has broken out their best crockery-- the stout, royal blue mugs embossed with the congressional seal, the chipped platter with the scalloped edges. He takes the platter in hand, offers cookies to the deacons.

"The senator must have been called in for a vote," Proctor says. "I'm sure he'll be along any moment now."

The Reverend Mr. Cleveland responds with a broad, indulgent smile. He sips his coffee. He sets the cup aside.

Ordinarily, Proctor would have long since plied them with apologies and earnest excuses and sent them on their way. But these are actual Negroes, three very black gentlemen. An honorable, ordained minister and two righteous deacons come to break bread with the senator and pray for his salvation.

Tillman can use them. He's been pawing the help again. A young woman from the slums of Anacostia has formally objected to the senator's attentions. She claims she was cleaning the toilet in his suite when the senator wandered in drunk and groped her.

Proctor has taken the usual measures--slyly, anonymously. Somehow the young woman's sealed police record has found its way into the press. Juvenile possession. Criminal solicitation. Somehow the father of her illegitimate children has flown in from South Carolina to speak publicly of her cocaine addiction, her tendency to lie.

And now actual Negroes, prepared to be seen and photographed with the senator, prepared to pray for his immortal soul. And prepared, Proctor has extracted from them, to believe that Tillman slipped on the soapy floor, to believe he tore that girl's blouse and dislodged her brassiere in a wholly innocent effort to stay upright.

Proctor checks his watch. He makes a mental note to ream Lewis.

Pam approaches from her desk. "Lewis on one."

Proctor stalks to his office. He shuts the door and snatches up the receiver.

"This'd better be good!"

Jack Proctor charges along a GWU medical center corridor, pursued by a receptionist.

"Sir. Sir! You're not allowed in here."

He ignores her. Out strides her. She throws up her hands and heads back toward the emergency waiting room with its ongoing insurrection.

Proctor sees Lewis at Tillman's bedside with a resident. He charges into the examination room.

"What in the shit happened!?"

He doesn't wait for a response.

"Senator, are you okay?"

Tillman tugs at his restraints.

"Liberarmi, per favore. Ho un` incarico."

Proctor turns to Lewis.

"What happened?"

"He just kind of went . . .nuts."

"Where's his goddamn hair!"

"Oh."

Lewis pulls the toupee from his pocket. He hands it to Proctor who steps to the bed and tries to situate it on Tillman's head.

Tillman grabs Proctor's arm. He pleads with him, whining pathetically.

"Devo trovare il mio condottiero."

Proctor jerks free, the toupee still in hand.

"What's he saying?"

"I'm told it's Italian, sir," Lewis volunteers.

"He wants you to unstrap him," the resident says. He draws a sedative into a syringe as he speaks. "He must seek his guide. He has a task. Something like that. My Italian's kind of rusty."

"A task?"

The resident nods. "He's been talking that way ever since he got here." He shows Proctor the hypodermic. "I want to knock him down a notch."

Proctor tosses the toupee to Lewis. "Make sure he wears this. This place'll be crawling with media."

Once the resident has drawn the needle from Tillman's arm, he and Proctor retire to the hallway. Lewis, vigilant by the bedside, watches Tillman fade into a narcotic stupor. "Mia lucertola. Mio condottiero."

As Tillman sags heavily onto the mattress, Lewis moves in with the toupee. He picks his opportunity and flings it onto Tillman's head. It's a clean shot, well aimed. Lewis admires his handiwork. Centered. Unmussed. Backwards.

Proctor and the intern peer in from the hallway through an observation window.

"What in the hell is going on?"

"Hard to say without further tests. We'll know more this evening."

As Proctor watches Tillman shift about on the bed, he sorts silently through the dire, potential consequences. The peril to the senator's committee chairmanship. The death of his legislative initiatives. His mysterious unavailability for *Meet the Press*.

"Has anything like this ever happened to him before?" the resident asks.

"Italian!? The man's from Kentucky, for Chrissakes. He barely speaks English."

14

In the farthest of the Renaissance Exhibition rooms, Beatrice and Ted stand before a large Veronese canvas. The fine, spring weather has thinned out the patrons, driven them onto the Mall and into the afternoon sun. A few dogged souls circulate past.

"See them?" Beatrice points toward the painting. "Lucertole. Condottieri."

"Lizards?"

Beatrice nods.

"Duane and I spent a heavenly week at the Gritti, but I didn't see one stinking lizard anywhere." Ted leans closer for a better look. "Cats," he says. "Lots of cats."

The painting depicts the return of the Doge Falieri from his triumph over the Dalmatians. He is stepping from the bucintoro-- his lavishly gilded barge -- onto the molo just before the twin columns.

His troops and his sailors have preceded him into the city. They have collected to greet him, their pikes lifted into the air. Venetian gentlemen, in brightly striped pantaloons and doublets, caper in the piazza. Priests kneel at the water's edge.

Falieri wears his zogia -- the jewel-encrusted cap of the doges. Hanging about his shoulders and draping full to the stones at his feet, is a richly embroidered cape of intricate design. Scarlet and yellow on a field of deepest black.

Ted leans close, and the pattern resolves. Lizards. Hundreds upon hundreds in thick array across the garment. Red tails and trunks, each pricked with yellow eyes.

"And not just any lizards," Beatrice says. "Condottieri di Falieri. Sangue lucertole. Falieri's generals. Blood lizards."

"Blood lizards?"

Beatrice nods.

"So what are you telling me? That moron Tillman is some sort of closet Venetian?"

Beatrice shrugs. "I don't know. It's just weird, that's all. I mean, how would Tillman know anything about this?"

"He probably threw a clot."

"But the guy's such a lug, and all of a sudden speaking fluent Italian. Creepy. Very creepy."

Doug planned on his pork chop fricassee. He purchased the ingredients at the store. He assembled them on the countertop. The yellow onion. The carrots. The dirt-flecked celery ribs. The garlic. The tomato paste. The hardy, non-potable burgundy. And a quartet of meaty loin chops.

He even began to heat a pan before he lost interest altogether. Chicken, he decided, extra crispy.

Upon his return, he finds that Jenny is shut away still in her room. He calls to her to let her know he's home.

"Okay," she shouts back, her voice stifled and muted by her bedroom door.

Jenny studies the scarlet lizard in the pickle jar on her desktop. It has eaten her bugs. It has discharged a filmy fluid that has dried and crusted over on the jar wall. It considers her back with its strange, yellow eyes.

She decides it will be pretty in with Sally, her iguana. The green and the red together. Sally will calm it, Jenny reasons. Sally will help it adjust to captivity.

Doug lays out the feast. The crusty chicken. The Styrofoam vat of coleslaw. The fist-sized biscuits. The coagulated gravy. The tub of reconstituted potatoes with the consistency of spackling.

"Soup's on."

"I'm coming."

He waits. He pours Jenny a tumbler of milk. He uncorks and sniffs the bottle of hardy, non-potable burgundy. He pours himself a glass and sips. It is definitely hardy. It is infinitely non-potable.

She's not coming.

"Jenny!"

Doug leaves the kitchen and passes through the dining room. He is mounting the stairs as Jenny rushes out of her room and draws shut her door behind her.

She bounces down the stairs, punching him in the stomach as she passes. She giggles and bolts through the dining room.

Up in her bedroom, there is the chatter already of claws frantic on glass. Sally, Jenny's iguana, throws herself at the wall of her terrarium with a meaty thump. She scratches wildly at the glass. She noses the screen-wire lid, desperate to escape.

The scarlet lizard perches upon the barkless fruitwood limb that is Sally's lone scrap of decor. It flicks its tongue with a gritty rasp as it eases onto the newsprint flooring.

Doug enters the kitchen to find Jenny spooning slaw onto her plate. She takes the merest spoonful of potatoes. A biscuit. A chicken leg. She plunges a plastic fork into the hardening gravy so that the hilt of it stands upright.

Doug sips his burgundy. It has been breathing in his glass on the table, and the flavor has altered dramatically. His hardy wine has become biting vinegar.

Doug dribbles his mouthful back into his glass.

"Daddy!! It's no wonder you can't get a date!"

"Who says I need a date?"

"Mom's been dead three years. It's time you moved on."

Doug nibbles at a thigh as he considers this morsel of advice. It sounds terribly familiar to him.

"You said Barbara was nice. Pretty. Interesting. Why don't you ask her out?"

"When exactly did I say all this?"

Jenny shifts in her chair. She concentrates intently on her chicken leg.

"You know. This morning. Sometime."

"Did you and Janice have a little chat?"

Jenny shifts uneasily in her seat.

"Maybe."

"And she told you all about Barbara?"

Jenny nods. "Janice said she was really pretty. She said she was smart and . . .outgoing."

Doug snorts. "She almost made my ears bleed."

"At least she's a grown up. I saw the way you were looking at that Amber girl. She's seventeen. I asked her. And she's an idiot."

"Excuse me!?"

"Oh, puhlease. A woman knows these things."

"You're ten!"

"It's that pierced belly button, isn't it? And the tan."

Doug can feel himself blushing. "That's ridiculous. She's my student!"

Jenny fairly cackles as she rises with her plate and scrapes it clean in the trash can.

"Are you finished?"

As best he can, Doug musters stock, parental concern. Of course she's finished. He knows she's finished.

Jenny crosses from the sink and kisses Doug on the cheek.

"Call Barbara. We think she's just right for you."

Doug watches Jenny stroll across the dining room, grinning at him mercilessly over her shoulder. She rounds the corner in the foyer, and scampers up the stairway.

Doug has hardly set about plotting revenge on Janice when Jenny screams. It is a piercing, desperate wail.

"Jenny!" Doug shouts, running already. "Jenny!"

He races up the stairs, reaching her winded, his heart pounding. She stands before Sally's terrarium, panting with sobs.

What little is left of Sally is scattered in grisly scraps about the enclosure. The glass walls are blood-splattered, entrail-smeared. A green scaly foot still twitches and trembles reflexively in a corner. Horny ridge spines litter the newsprint flooring. A pale sliver of underbelly drifts lazily in the water dish.

Doug draws Jenny to him. She is quivering. Only then does he see it. Hidden at first beneath the fruitwood limb, it scampers topside and slips into the light.

"What in the hell is that!?"

"I found him," Jenny blubbers.

Doug eases closer for a better look. He's never seen a creature remotely like it. Red, of all things. And with searing, yellow eyes.

"Where?"

"On the Mall. I was going to tell you."

"Let's get him out of here and clean this up. Where's your jar?"

Jenny fetches for Doug her specimen jar. Mt. Olive Pickle chips. He unscrews the punctured lid. Using a pair of pencils as makeshift chop sticks, Doug reaches toward the lizard. The creature squirms unnervingly as Doug lifts it by the trunk and transfers it to the jar. He screws down the lid.

Doug eyes the lizard and taps the glass with his finger. The gullet distends. The jaws hinge open.

Three doors away, in a clapboard split level, a woman quarreling with her husband over money, interrupts a pointed accusation to ask him, "What in the living hell was that?"

15

Beatrice waits at the counter, just by the candy rack. Tony is busy with a customer -- a willowy brunette in running shoes and maroon, Lycra tights. Beatrice looks her up and down. She is infuriatingly svelte.

The brunette pays for her small bottle of sparkling water. Tony counts out her change. She lingers still to chat. She has lately read a book she is terribly keen on, a touching novel about a man who communicates telepathically with dogs. She acquaints Tony with the plot in scrupulous detail.

Beatrice simmers. She shifts from one foot to the other in her baggy gray sweat suit, her shabby canvas shoes.

The brunette giggles. She glances at Beatrice. "I talk too much," she says.

Tony reaches under the counter and pulls out Beatrice's *Il Gazzettino*. Her *La Republica*. He hands them to her, shoving them past Barbara who has set in on her paraphrase of the stirring schnauzer interlude.

She pauses long enough to grin at Beatrice and tell her brightly, "Ciao."

Beatrice glances at the front page of her *Il Gazzettino* on the sidewalk outside. The news from Venice is lively and arresting.

A German tourist has died under curious circumstances in the courtyard of the Doge's Palace. Facts are scarce. Poison is a possibility. Deadly nightshade is suspected.

There is, as well, a photograph of a Falieri. Matteo. He is prominent below the fold. An odd little man with sharp Venetian features. The bold accompanying headline catches Beatrice's eye:

Il Morte in La Venezia! Death in Venice.

Beatrice reads the article beneath a lamppost on Wisconsin. In the Italian way, it is shrill and turgid. It is frankly sentimental. It is lightly littered with facts.

She learns of a cold-blooded murder in the city. A grocery clerk -- an Antonio Steno -- has been dispatched with a knife. Barely thirty and blameless, he was butchered on a fine spring morning. And not merely a murder, Beatrice reads, but also a suicide. Strangely ritualistic. Utterly Mystifying.

Falieri.

She studies the picture again.

Steno.

Even with her newspapers flapping beneath her arm and her door key pricking her instep, Beatrice overtakes three authentic and impeccably turned out joggers. She sprints headlong past them down 30th Street on her way home. She lays the *Il Gazzettino* article out before her on her dinette. She retrieves books from her shelves, everything she can find that touches on Venice.

Her Calvino. Her Ruskin. Her Baron Corvo. A couple of dry histories of the empire. Assorted travelogues. Art surveys. A hotel guide. Her Michelin. She knows she's seen those names in tandem. She has read them paired together before. Falieri and Steno. She can't place just where.

Beatrice scours through indexes. She sifts through entire texts. She finds mere lines here and there devoted to Doge Marino Falieri. She strays across the odd and inconsequential Steno.

Her Michelin sends her to a travelogue, which delivers her to Ruskin. She drifts deeply into a catalog from Ca' d'Oro. She reads closely fully half of her

62

Calvino. Then back to her Michelin, and there they are. Her eye picks them out as she rifles through the pages.

A stray paragraph buried deep within a prose tour of the Piazza San Marco.

It is a terse account of the fate of Marino Falieri. In 1355, at the age of seventy-two, he took a young woman from Murano for his bride. Little more than twenty, she was a creature of exceptional beauty and stark faithlessness. She betrayed Falieri with a Steno, a young aristocrat. He carved a lewd poem in her honor into Falieri's ducal throne.

Provoked and humiliated, Falieri plotted to murder Steno. He conspired with his privy attendants and select of his palace guards who had their own complaints against boorish young bluebloods of the Republic.

Falieri proposed they round them up and kill them all. He found them vulgar, these young men. He thought them entirely expendable. And he might have succeeded if a ducal guard hadn't betrayed him to the council.

Falieri was condemned and beheaded on the Giants' Stairway. His conspirators were flayed and hanged, two to a ledge, from the windows of the Doge's Palace.

Beatrice shuts her Michelin and sits for a moment, weighing what she knows. First Tillman babbling in Italian on the Mall. His lizard. His guide. And now a Falieri brings death to a Steno. Not hotly, though. Without trace of feuding passion. Just quickly and neatly of a fine spring morning. Almost surgically.

She stands and crosses to the mahogany china cupboard in the far corner. Beatrice carefully opens the fragile arched door with its rickety mullions and its rattling glass. There between her ivory antelope and her plump jade dove sits the creature her mother owned as a child on Murano.

They were once common mementos of trips to Venice. That would be before chrome lighters engraved with the Campanile. Velour gondolier slippers in unspeakable colors. T-shirts embossed on the front with a view of the Piazza, on the back with "I'm With Stupido".

Beatrice's scarlet glass lizard has been mended twice. As a child, her mother snapped a foot off and reattached it badly. But the break in the delicate, tail was repaired by Beatrice's father. He was stingy with the epoxy. He left the faintest of fracture lines.

Beatrice takes up the telephone receiver and dials her parents' number.

"Ciao, Mom. Got a minute?"

Beatrice lightly runs her fingertip along the lizard's dusty spine.

"Good. Listen, I just came across that lizard you gave me. The glass one. I can't quite remember the story that goes with it."

Beatrice's mother lapses into Italian.

"Falieri, si." Beatrice settles onto the couch, drawing her feet beneath her.

"Si, la vendetta," Beatrice says, nodding. "That's it. Dieci da dieci." Ten by ten.

16

It is dusky midnight at Cape Farewell on the southern tip of Greenland. A quartet of French geologists drinks calvados in a flimsy, prefab cabin.

The swirling arctic wind tries the joints and seams. It rattles the lone door and the pair of tiny windows. It sluices through the stovepipe and blows ash and stray live coals onto the floor.

The men are weary. Drunk. They discuss French politics earnestly. They smoke. The oldest of them rises from the table, which is littered still with dishes and the leavings of dinner.

He is whiskery and bald. He is arthritic and ailing. He is oblivious and slack-jawed.

He has heard his name.

He must go.

The others, at first, are content to believe that he has parked himself in the outhouse or is gathering wood from their snow-dusted stash. But when nearly an hour has passed and he has still not returned, they step out into the bright midnight to seek him.

He is but a speck to the east against the snow pack. He moves slowly but relentlessly, slogging through the drifts.

It clings to an ice-scarred rock by the shoreline. Arrestingly red in that monochromatic landscape. Its raspy tongue darts and probes. Its yellow eyes glow.

17

Beatrice races up the Gallery steps in the morning light. She neglects the Venetian masters. She proceeds directly through the rotunda and into the administrative suite beyond. She enters her office, tosses her satchel on the floor, and sits at her cluttered desk.

Beatrice feels about for her laptop computer beneath heaps of paperwork and piles of museum catalogs. She finds it and drags it out into the light.

Beatrice maneuvers her way into an Italian index in Milan. Keyword: Falieri. She scrolls and reads. With growing excitement. With accumulating alarm.

Beatrice prints out a couple of close-typed pages. She takes her *Il Gazzettino* and the morning edition of The Washington Times from her satchel. She charges into the hallway.

She is shouting already, "Ted!" before she is well through her doorway.

Ted's office is tidy and inviting. It is an evolving decorating project. A schizophrenic, personal statement. Deco. Empire. Queen Anne. Stickley. Jetsons.

Ted sits at his desk trying to print an address on an envelope. He consults his computer user guide.

"I've upgraded my template. I've selected 'envelopes and labels'."

He enters a command on his keyboard.

"Now print."

Nothing.

"Ted!"

"Print!"

66

Nothing. He removes his shoe. Ted is clubbing his monitor with the heel of it as Beatrice charges in from the hallway.

"You are never going to believe this!" she says.

"Would you please tell me how to make this thing. . . "

Beatrice slaps down the newspapers on the blotter before him. "Look at this." She taps the photo of Matteo Falieri.

"Sugar, I'm right in the middle of a psychotic episode. In the name of sweet Jesus, what is mail merge!?"

"Look at it!" Beatrice smacks her open palm on the desktop.

"It's always you, you, you, isn't it?"

"Humor me."

"Okay. But when we finish with you, I get my snit. Agreed?"

"Fine."

Ted looks. "You know my Italian's shaky."

"It's an article about a murder in Venice. A Falieri killed a Steno and then killed himself."

"A what?"

"A Falieri! Like the doge, in the painting. Remember?

"Right. Falieri."

"Now look at this."

Beatrice lays before him the pages from her printer. Ted studies them, squinting over the miniscule print. They are also in Italian.

"Precisely ten years ago another Falieri killed another Steno in Maestre, on the mainland."

She shifts over to the second page and points to another passage.

"And ten years before that, in Bergamo. Another murder suicide. A Falieri and a Steno."

"Maybe they're just the Hatfields and McCoys of the Veneto."

"And look at this."

Beatrice taps with her finger on the *Il Gazzettino* below the fold. She indicates the brief article about the German tourist poisoned in the inner courtyard of the Doge's palace. She reads through it, translating for Ted.

"They suspect belladonna in some highly toxic concentrate. How he came across it, particularly in the Palazzo Ducale, nobody can figure out. And then there's this."

Beatrice shifts the Il Gazzettino aside to reveal the Washington Times.

"You read that rag!"

Beatrice flips the paper over. She points out a photo of Senator Royce Tillman. It's an airbrushed campaign portrait with the unfurled flag for a background.

"They're saying he hurt his knee playing softball."

"What did you expect? 'He had a Mediterranean, nervous breakdown?'

"Don't you think this is all a little too weird?" All of these Falieris and Stenos! This poisoned German! And now Tillman!"

"What's Tillman got to do with all of these other guys. In fact, what have all these other guys got to do with each other?"

"Three times in thirty years, a Falieri has killed a Steno. Just out of the blue and for no reason. In the fourteenth century, the Doge Marino Falieri conspired to kill a Michele Steno. That's how he got beheaded. That's why he was disgraced. That's why his portrait in the Doge's Palace is painted over with a veil."

Beatrice fishes an item from her jacket pocket. It is wrapped in tissue. She pulls away the Kleenex to reveal her scarlet glass lizard. She sets it gingerly on Ted's desk.

"Where'd you get that?"

"From my mom. It's a . . ."

"I know, I know. His lizard. His guide."

Ted exhales conspicuously.

68

"Honey, you know I love you, but magic lizards! Is that where we're going with this?"

"Remember that night you saw Jesse Helms on your terrace? I believed you."

"That was different!"

Ted plucks the glass lizard off his desktop. He settles it gently upon his palm.

"It was my mother's when she was a little girl. I talked to her last night. She told me the whole story about Falieri's execution. I'm starting to think this is all tied together."

Ted moans. "You're not up on the grassy knoll again are you?"

"Just listen for a minute, will you?"

Sullenly, Ted wets his finger with his tongue and dabs dust out of the bends and recesses of the glass lizard.

"What do you know about negromanzia--black magic? Curses?"

"Do you mean like . . .?" Ted wriggles his fingers at Beatrice. He gives her the evil eye.

She nods.

"Well. I know a curse is just a wish your heart makes."

"I believe that's 'a dream'."

Bobbing his head, his lips moving ever so slightly, Ted works his way well into the Disney songbook.

"Oh. Right."

"It turns out that Doge Falieri was very deep into the black arts. He was a notorious conjurer. It was thought that he could summon demons."

Beatrice draws Ted's Biedermeier side chair to his desk. She perches upon it, pitched forward.

"He was renowned for his powers. Was said to have called in a plague on the Dalmatians."

"Beety, it was the fourteenth century, for Godsakes. Those people thought the earth was flat."

"According to legend, the city of Venice was founded at the stroke of noon on the twenty-fifth of March in 421 A.D.. Marino Falieri and his nine co-conspirators were executed at dawn on the twenty-fifth of March in 1350. The twenty-fifth of March was three days ago."

"That I'll give you."

"The legend holds that Falieri vowed vengeance. Right there on the Giants' Stairway. Just before he was beheaded. Ten by ten."

"Excuse me?"

"Dieci da dieci. And then people started turning up dead. Ten killed by ten, once every ten years. That's one death for each conspirator."

"But Beety . . ."

"Do the math. This would be a tenth year." Beatrice snatches up her *Il Gazzettino* and waves it under Ted's nose. "Don't you see, it's old guys killing young guys. That's just what Falieri's wanted."

"And the lizards?"

"His emmissaries. His . . . familiars. You heard Tillman. His lizard. His guide. Somehow, he was selected."

"Tillman!? By a lizard!? How!?"

"I don't know. Maybe there's Venetian blood in his line."

"So if Tillman gets his lizard, like he wants, he's going to kill some other slob who doesn't know he's a Venetian?"

Beatrice shrugs a little helplessly and nods.

"What kind of hare-brained curse is that? And nobody's noticed but you!?"

"Who would!? Especially now. I'll bet ten people are killed every other day in D.C. alone."

"You can't possibly believe this."

"There is a way we can find out exactly what's going on, if anything."

70

Beatrice eases close to Ted's desk to acquaint him
with her plan.

"Hold it," Ted says. "I'm not going to get my snit,
am I?"

18

Jenny awoke anxious for him to kill it. Desperate to drown the wicked creature in their toilet, but Doug decided instead to carry it to school. Identify it in a field guide during study hall. Offer it to Nelson, his buddy at the zoo.

Doug can't seem, however, to find it in his books. He comes across a gecko native to Maritius. Its hide is knobby and scarlet-speckled but on a field of moldy aquamarine. The red-tinged squamata from the Sinai looks to Doug a little closer in color. But it's too plump and tends toward stripes. Its tail is spiny and unusually stubby.

Doug briefly wonders if his lizard might have been dyed, like a parakeet. But the line where the red skin fades to pale underbelly looks too artful and organic for that. The best he can do, with all his field guides and textbooks open before him, is a southern European wall lizard. Podarcis Muralis.

The scale and shape are right. The color and the pattern are given as variable. The snout is appropriately tapered and pointed. The tail, aptly, extends well beyond body length.

Doug allows that the coloring on Jenny's skink could merely be freakish. Genetically accidental. The thing might have been flushed down a condo toilet and survived its trip along the waist drain. It could have hissed once too often and gotten freed onto the Mall.

Podarcis Muralis. Doug is largely satisfied.

He looks about his classroom. He'd welcome a second opinion. But of the four students in his study hall, three are profoundly asleep.

The fourth one, Mr. Tilley, chews a scrap of loose leaf paper. A perennial trade-school hopeful, he's hunched over his desk jotting the answers to an upcoming geography test on his palm. The elevation of Lima. Three tributaries of the Amazon. The capitals of Suriname and Paraguay.

Doug sees Janice pass in the corridor on her way to the lounge. Her empty mug in hand. The inner, un-read sections of the *Post* under her arm.

He catches up with her at the lounge door.

"Janice, come here a minute. I want you to look at my lizard."

Janice lays a fluttering hand to the base of her neck. She bats her eyelids. Her chocolate Blanche Dubois. "Why Mr. Gunther, whatever do you mean?"

She permits him to drive her before him into his classroom. Eagle-eyed, Janice pauses along the aisle by Mr. Tilley's desk.

"Victor, it's Asuncion."

"Huh?" Mr. Tilley peers up at her with his customary slackened grain-fed expression.

"The capital of Paraguay. A-s-u-n-c-i-o-n. Accent over the "o"."

Janice continues up the aisle. Mr. Tilley sweats profusely. His scholarship smudges. It drains along the creases of his palm.

"Now that's a lizard." Janice bends to peer into the jar. "Hank used to have a Pontiac that color."

Doug hands her a field guide. It is open to a photograph of Podarcis Muralis.

"What do you think? Him?"

"Maybe."

Janice reads the entry by the photo.

"Southeastern Europe and Asia?"

Doug nods. "I'm figuring him for an escapee."

"Where'd you get him?"

"Jenny found him, on the Mall."

Janice bends again to look at the lizard. Doug circles around from behind his desk and steps toward the classroom door.

"Where are you going?" Janice asks him.

"I want to call Nelson. The snake guy. See if he wants him."

"Jenny's not going to keep it?"

Doug shakes his head. "It ate her iguana."

"Now why in the world did you do that?" Janice says, tapping with her fingernail on the glass.

The gullet distends. The jaws hinge open.

All four of Doug's students sit bolt upright, jolted awake by the hiss. Janice cowers by the wall, pressed against Doug's corkboard. His memos and directives. His "Deadly Serpents of the World" calendar opened prematurely to April--Australian Death Adder.

In a back room of the reptile house at the D.C. Zoo, Doug's buddy Nelson fills an eyedropper with antibiotics and squirts the dose into the mouth of an Asian rock python.

He ignores for the moment the ringing telephone. He strokes the massive snake's head. He leans down to give the snake a little peck on the snout.

Nelson reaches for the phone receiver.

"Hey, Dougie. Where've you been keeping yourself?"

As he talks, Nelson drags the python across the examination table, struggling against its lethargic bulk.

"What kind of lizard? Yeah, it happens. They get here by hook or crook. I once found a double-crested basilisk in South Carolina. Go figure."

Nelson wrestles the python into its tank, folding its length upon itself.

"Red? Well, that is a little odd. Uh huh. Uh huh."

He gives the python a fond pat and settles the mesh lid on top of its tank.

"Yeah, sure. I'll take him off your hands. I'll be at a conference in Philly for the next couple of days. Why don't you bring him by on Friday. We can go for a beer or something."

Nelson sniffs at the musk on his hands, plainly enjoying the stink.

"A whole iquana!? Then that's no wall lizard. I don't know off hand, but just keep him in the jar until you bring him in. Good. Good. Okay, I'll see you then."

Nelson hangs up the receiver. "Ate an iguana," he says, shaking his head. He steps toward the door, passing a knobby desert horned viper, which coils and strikes, thumping its snout against its terrarium glass.

19

Senator Royce Tillman has commanded a sunny, private corner room in a quiet wing of the GWU hospital. Lewis sits in an armchair, shifting among chirpy hostesses on mid-morning TV gabfests. He's been there all night. Lewis still has on his jacket and khakis. His loosened power tie.

Tillman jerks his tethered arms. He rattles the bedrails. He moans and complains in slurred, sedated Italian. "Mia lucertola. Mio condottiero. Ho un` incarico."

Lewis raises the remote and turns up the TV. He watches a brunette on the Baltimore station. She oversees a decorating demonstration and manages bubbly enthusiasm for wall stenciling.

Tillman rattles his bedrails. Again, he bucks his toupee. As Lewis settles it back onto his scalp, Tillman grabs him by the blazer.

"Liberarmi, per favore! Liberarmi!"

By the time Lewis has worked himself free, Proctor has already escorted the senator's wife into the room.

Her hair is sandy and artfully highlighted. Her dress is tailored and snug. She has been tucked and tautened. She pauses to study Lewis with a frankly predatory gaze.

Delores Tillman drops her handbag on a chair seat. She takes in the room. She crinkles her nose at the hospital stink as she approaches her husband's bedside and peers down at him.

He writhes. He struggles against his tethers. "Liberarmi, per favore. Ho un` incarico!"

Lewis stands by to be handy in case she's overcome with emotion. She only shakes her head. She turns briefly toward Lewis. She eyes him again, slowly along his length.

"What the hell's wrong with him?"

She's looking at Lewis. She's talking to Proctor.

"They're not sure."

"What's he saying?"

"It's Italian. Something about his lizard."

She shrieks with laughter. Lewis can hardly believe it.

"His lizard!"

She produces a pack of Winstons from the pocket of her suit jacket and lights one. As Delores Tillman blows smoke through her nose, she reaches to smooth and straighten Lewis' jacket lapel.

"The doctor thinks he might have had a . . . brain episode," Proctor says. "They're still running tests. We'll know more this afternoon."

"Fine," she says. Delores plucks her purse off the chair seat. "Call me."

"Delores, wait."

Proctor steps into the doorway, blocking her way.

"I'm going with arthoscopic surgery. A knee. Torn ligaments."

"How? Falling off a cocktail waitress?"

"We've got a lot to lose here. If those jackals on the Hill find out what kind of shape he's in, we're in trouble. No chairmanship. No E.P.A. legislation. No block-grant bill. No re-election. No nothing."

"You mean you've got a lot to lose."

"Royce needs you. I need you."

She smokes languorously, wandering the room. "How did he hurt it?" she asks at last.

"Softball. Out in Middleburg with the Tillman clan."

"Very Kennedy."

"That's the idea."

"So I'm concerned, but I have every reason to be hopeful?"

Proctor nods. "And you don't know how long he'll be laid up," he instructs her.

"When and where?"

"I'll call downstairs and tell them to set up in the parking lot. You stop on your way out. You make a statement. You take a couple of questions. That's it."

"What do I get?"

"What do you want?"

Delores weighs her prospects. She glances about the room. Her gaze settles on Lewis.

"He's a new one, isn't he?"

"Yeah. Lewis, say hello to Mrs. Tillman."

"Hi."

She smiles at Lewis. She draws open his blazer. "What are you, thirty-four in the waist?"

"I'm thirty-two, ma'm."

She drags her fingers along his chest. "Do you lift weights, Lewis?"

"Sometimes, ma'm. I jog."

"How old are you?"

"I'm nineteen, ma'm."

"I'll bet you can just jog, and jog, and jog."

"Yes ma'm. I do about five miles a day."

Delores Tillman brushes his hair back with her fingers. She winks at Lewis. She turns toward Proctor. "Wrap him up."

Lewis can see her through the tinted limousine window. She stands before a thicket of microphones in the hospital parking lot. Proctor hovers close at her elbow, smiling as he watches her speak. She dabs at her nose with a tissue.

Proctor steers her away from the microphones. He squires her by the elbow to her car. She slips onto the seat beside Lewis.

"I'll call you when I need you," Proctor tells him.

"Yes sir."

He shuts the door.

"To the apartment, Mrs. Tillman?"

It's the driver. The back of his head anyway. His eyes in the rearview mirror.

"No, Robert. We're going to the country."

"Yes ma'm."

Delores toggles a switch and raises the partition behind the driver's seat. She rests her hand high along Lewis' thigh. "I'm so upset about Royce," she says and lays her head upon his shoulder.

"Yes ma'm."

She brushes her lips against his neck. She smells of tobacco, of talcum and Final Net. "There's just no telling what I might do."

20

Frail, silver-haired, pallid -- a man stands in the lobby of a central London office tower in his damp loden topcoat. The slender blade of a stiletto --nearly invisible on edge--extends from one hand. The other runs with blood. Onto the skirt of his coat. Onto the cuff of his trouser leg. Onto the cleft slate floor.

A young executive drops toward the street in an elevator car. His secretary shoves documents at him.

"Sign here, Mr. Parker," she instructs him. "Initials here."

Mr. Parker obliges and then checks his reflection in the brass elevator wall. The hang of his suit. The lay of his hair. The beguiling charm of his smile.

The lobby guard -- bored, Senegalese-- flips through his copy of *The Sun* at the station by the elevator banks.

He glances again at the old man across the lobby. Pale. Waiting. Standing stiffly before the tapestry hanging from the far wall. He looks harmless enough.   The express elevator doors slide open, and Mr. Parker charges out of the car and across the lobby. His secretary hurries along behind him, her heels clicking on the tiles.

"So that's a no on the Prince's Trust?" she asks.

"Just send the fool a check."

"And the Royal Shakespeare?"

"Same."

The silver-haired man in the damp loden coat steps between Mr. Parker and the doorway to the street.

"Ah," he says, "signore."

"Sir, I'm sorry, but Mr. Parker is hardly available for. . ."

80

The man swings his arm and sends the secretary skidding across the lobby. Interested now, the guard rises.

"Per i suoi delitti."

"Say bloody what!?" Mr. Parker shouts just as the silver-haired man pricks him neatly twice.

Young Mr. Parker jerks and twitches as if stung. He cries out.

The Senegalese guard, armed only with a lacquered length of ash, approaches slowly, carefully. He is relieved to see the blade slipped between the ribs and pressed home.

Mr. Parker lies on his back. He is wet and cold. He is sleepy. He is safe now. They watch over him from above. The black man with the lacquered cudgel. The woman who can't stop screaming.

21

Ted and Beatrice ride up Virginia Avenue in Ted's
immaculate Saab, negotiating their way through sluggish
mid-afternoon traffic. Ted turns right onto 22nd Street.
He finds a spot by the curb a mere block from the
hospital. They climb out of the car and walk north
toward Pennsylvania Avenue.

"What are you going to say to him?" Ted asks.

Beatrice shrugs. "Maybe he did throw off a clot.
Maybe I'm wrong. How else am I going to find out?"

"And you think they're just going to let us in!?"

They round a corner and draw in sight of the
G.W.U. Medical Center.

"That's where you come in."

The lobby of the admitting wing is divided neatly
and conspicuously into classes. There is steerage over by
the regular desk. It is the spot for mere mortals with its
puckering wood-grained lamination and matched set of
plump, admitting nurses in their starched white uniforms,
their pink cardigans.

Relatives of patients in leisurewear plead for the
tattered, purple passes that will admit them to the upper
floors.

Well across the lobby and fully segregated from the
riff raff, the admitting desk of the Mellon Pavilion is an
elegant study in quarried stone. Behind it stands a doe-
eyed young woman with flowing hair and a lanky, angular
build perfectly suited to her clingy cocktail dress.

Her telephone pulses pleasingly with each incoming
call. She fields questions and dispenses information with
cordial patience and breathy sympathy. To the occasional
guest she presents passes to the Mellon Pavilion Tower

that are the size of silver dollars. They are made of hand-worked tongue-oiled koa wood from the upland groves of Oahu.

Ted and Beatrice linger near the entranceway to formulate a strategy. Ted considers the lanky receptionist. He glances at Beatrice, weighing their options. Ted draws his silk handkerchief from the breast pocket of his blazer and snaps it open.

"Here." He hands it to Beatrice. "Tie this around your head."

Beatrice, not given to head scarves, folds the handkerchief poorly and ties it worse.

"No, no, no! Not like a Ukranian. With some style! And put these on."

Ted gives Beatrice his sunglasses. She slips them on and adjusts her head scarf. Ted steps back to take her in.

From the neck up --with the kerchief and the glasses-- she looks a little like a continental starlet of the sixties. From the neck down --in her untailored, earth-tone dress and sturdy shoes -- she looks very much like a heartland librarian.

"That'll have to do. Have you got a Kleenex?"

Beatrice produces a frayed tissue from her pocket.

"You're upset. You're crying."

Beatrice makes a show of tears.

"When I call you over, you only speak Italian. You don't understand English. Capice?"

"Certo."

Ted pauses to button his jacket. He musses his hair to fall at a rakish angle. He smiles and advances toward the Mellon Pavilion reception desk.

There is no line. There is no waiting. The receptionist beams fondly at him as he closes upon the desk. "Welcome to the Mellon Pavilion. How may I help you?"

"Ciao, bella."

Ted speaks with a lilting mongrel-European accent, a Mediterranean patois.

"I am the Marquis di Laguna. But please to call me Teodore." Ted takes the receptionist by the fingers and lightly shakes her hand as he clicks his heels together and bows.

"Ashley," she says.

"Ah, bellissima."

"Do you wish to visit a guest?"

"Ah, yes, a guest. We have come to pay a call on the Senator Mr. Tillman."

Ashley glances about the lobby.

"We?"

"It is, how you say, complicated. Permit me to explain. Ted cuts his eyes suspiciously. He leans in to speak discreetly to Ashley. He motions for her to draw close. "Do you see the young lady there?"

Ted points toward Beatrice. She dabs at her nose. Quivers persuasively. Ashley nods.

"She is the Senator Mr. Tillman's daughter." Ted is whispering now.

Ashley checks her leather-bound, Mellon Pavilion reception book. She flips through it to the Tillman entry. Scans the page.

"I don't show a daughter, Mister . . uh . . Laguna."

"Teodore. I am insisting."

"We have no record of the senator having a daughter, Teodore."

"Yes, precisely. As is also true of Mrs. Senator Royce Tillman."

Ashely smiles, baffled.

"Some years ago, the senator was quite the . . .how you say. . .man of the ladies. You take my meaning?"

Ashley nods.

"Many, many lovers. Many, many affairs of the heart. And without consequence, but for Sophia. She was . . . especially fertile."

"Sophia?"

"Sophia Loren. You know her, no?"

Ashley shakes her head.

84

"How to describe Sophia. In Italy, my home, she is like your J-Lo, but with . . ."

As Ted gropes for a word, he curls his fingers and cups his hands before his chest.

"Implants?" Ashley offers.

"No, no, no." Ted ponders. "Ah, yes. Talent."

Ashley shuts her leather-bound log.

"Well, I'm sorry, but I can't just let you . . ."

"They are so very close --the senator and his daughter-- and she will need but a moment."

"I'm afraid I'm not allowed to . . ."

"Because tomorrow, if she finds the senator strong and well, she will bring her half-brother for a visit. Mr. Clooney."

"George?"

"Naturalmente. Sophia, she was, how you say, generous.

"She's going to bring George Clooney here!?"

"He should meet you, bellissima. His love life, it is . ." Ted shakes his head. Grimaces.

Ashley reconsiders. She opens her ledger.

"Fifteen minutes. That's the best I can do."

Ted beckons Beatrice. She approaches, dabbing her nose.

"Si, bella. Quindici minuti."

Beatrice arrives at the desk. She smiles uneasily at Ashley who hands over a pair of koa-wood, tongue-oiled passes.

"Eighth floor."

Ashley points out the waiting elevator, its hammered bronze doors standing open.

"You are so very kind, Signora Ashley. We thank you. Sophia thanks you."

Ted fondly lays his arm around Beatrice.

"Andiamo. Questa via."

He ushers her into the elevator car. Dabbing at her nose still, Beatrice rests her head on his shoulder. She speaks softly into his ear.

"What is that accent? Zorro?"
The heavy, dimpled doors glide shut.

The elevator doors slide open on the eighth floor.
Berber carpet. Glazed terra-cotta tile border. The smell
of lilac. Jasmine.
Ted and Beatrice step from the car. They look up
and down the hallway. They strike out away from the
nurses' station.
Beatrice and Ted pass the door to the solarium.
They pause to peek inside. A violinist plays.
Ambulatory patients and guests enjoy a buffet lunch.
The room suggests the promenade deck of a cruise ship.
More White Star Line than Carnival.
"Hear him?"
Ted stops to listen.
"Liberarmi! Liberarmi!"
They follow the sound of Tillman's voice. The door
to his room stands open. He is quite alone.
"I'll keep an eye out," Ted says.
Beatrice enters the room. Tillman is a pathetic sight.
He shifts about sluggishly in the bed, tethered to the
railings at his wrists and ankles. He has shed his toupee
onto his pillow. His gown --rich Mellon Pavilion flannel
but still open at the back -- has crept up revealingly. As
Beatrice reaches to tug it down, Tillman grabs her arm.
"Liberarmi, per favore. Ho un` incarico."
"A task?"
"Liberarmi!"
"Quale incarico?"
"La vendetta. La vendetta."
Beatrice looks toward Ted, lingering in the doorway.
"Are you getting this? He says he has a task. I ask
him what it is, and he says 'vengeance'."
Beatrice turns again t Tillman. "La vendetta per
Falieri?"
Tillman smiles rapturously. His eyes well with tears.
"Mio padrone!"

"Il Doge Falieri?"

"Mio principe!"

"His master," she says to Ted. "His prince."

Ted makes a sly, vigorous motion for Beatrice to join him in the hall. "Here comes a nurse."

As Beatrice leaves Tillman's bedside, he begins to shriek. "Liberarmi, per favore! Ho un` incarico! Liberarmi!" He jerks at his restraints. Rattles the rails.

"Cry," Ted hisses at Beatrice as she joins him the doorway, and she buries her face in her hands, sobbing convincingly. Ted ushers past the oncoming nurse. He escorts her into the elevator car.

Together Ted and Beatrice exit the lobby of the medical center. Beatrice looses the knot of Ted's handkerchief and works the thing off of her head.

"So what are we going do?"

Ted shrugs. "What can we do?"

"We've got to tell somebody. You heard him. His master. His prince. La vendetta."

"I can't for the life of me figure out how a curse could possibly work. I don't even know how my microwave works."

"Maybe it just works because it works. Maybe there's more going on in this life than we've ever imagined. Above it. Beneath it. Behind it. Invisible to us."

"Nobody's going to believe you. You know that don't you? It's not like you can go to the cops with this."

"So you're not going to help me?"

"Help you what?"

"I want to find that lizard. Tillman's lizard."

"How?"

"You heard him. 'Piccina, viene qua.' Little girl, come back."

"Yeah, but what little girl?"

"I don't know, but she got on that bus. The Fighting Maurauders. I remember that. It was one of

87

those schools in the burbs. Nathan Hale. Aaron Burr. Somebody."

"Aaron Burr?"

"Are you going to help me or not?"

"You know me," Ted tells her as he fishes his keys from his trouser pocket. He presses a button on the fob, and his Saab, hard by the curb before them, beeps and coos. "I give," he says. "And I give. Then I give some more."

22

The Gunther house is dark. The neighborhood quiet but for a hound up the block. Barking. Grumbling. Mouthing intermittently at the moon.

The blue wash from the vapor light on the street pours in through the windows of Doug's den. It falls in latticed patches on the floor and the settee. On the shelving along the wall -- on the outdated World Book Encyclopedias. The National Geographics. Gail's college art texts. Doug's dusty LPs.

A streak of cool blue lamplight bisects Doug's desktop. His satchel sits open on the blotter between a stack of thermofaxed pop quizzes and Jenny's pickle jar with its perforated lid.

The punctures are the girth of a ten-penny nail. Large enough to accommodate a trio of lizard claws. Scaly and scarlet, they emerge through a hole at the outer edge of the lid. They curl over the torn and upflung metal. They shift the lid in its threads.

The lid raises but a slight and tinny clatter as it skids across the blotter and drops onto the carpeted floor. The scarlet lizard, its yellow eyes aglow, scuttles over the jar rim onto the desk. Up the wall. Around to the near window where it tests the fit of the sash with the sill.

It tries the hole where the TV coax passes through the wallboard -- caulked. Where the front door meets the threshold -- weather-stripped and snug. Where the living-room chimney damper stoppers up the flue. The half-bath exhaust vent. The basement door. The range hood. The kitchen drain.

Foiled by aggressive suburban energy efficiency, the red lizard lingers briefly on the foyer rug before darting up the newel post and scampering along the varnished banister toward the upper floor. Where Jenny sleeps deeply on her back. Where Doug twitches beneath his bedclothes, dreaming.

The sky is a brilliant blue. The stadium is filled to capacity. Seven shirtless men in the front row, with green letters painted on their chests, rise together and sneeze in unison. They spell out the word 'globule'.

Doug stands on the sideline with Mr. Perry Como.

"Nice outfit," Perry says.

Doug wears a pair of his father's Sans-a-Belt slacks. A pleated blouse he was always fond of on Gail. His mother's brother's sweat-stained pork-pie hat. It is just what he intended to wear.

"Thank you," he says.

A color guard enters the stadium and marches the length of the field. It is comprised of three men in Romulan body armor and paper food-service hats. Each man carries a blue flag with a green hummingbird on it. The color guard stops in the far end zone and turns, high-stepping, to face mid-field.

Perry Como kisses Doug upon each cheek. He pats Doug's backside. "Be sweet," he says.

Doug salutes Mr. C and trots onto the field. He approaches a microphone stand at the center of the mid-field stripe. The fans rise, as one, to their feet, cheering.

The crowd falls silent. Doug taps on the microphone. He begins to sing.

"John Jacob Jingleheimer Schmidt. His name is my name too. Whenever we go out, the people always shout, 'There goes John Jacob Jingleheimer Schmidt."

The fans thunder, "Da da da da da da da."

Doug sings again, more softly now. "John Jacob Jingleheimer Schmidt. His name is my name too. . ."

In the end zone, a member of the color guard grows uneasy. He waves his hummingbird flag violently. He flings his flagstaff to the ground and runs toward Doug.

". . .Whenever we go out, the people always shout, 'There goes John Jacob Jingleheimer Schmidt.'"

Doug sees the man running, waving his arms. His paper hat flies from his head. His Romulan body armor chatters as he runs.

The crowed thunders, "Da da da da da da da."

Doug is down to a whisper. "John Jacob Jingleheimer Schmidt, his name is my name too. . ."

Wild-eyed and frantic, the man draws up directly before Doug and stops. He salutes. Doug falls silent.

The man opens his mouth and speaks, oddly, with the voice of a child. A familiar voice. A familiar child. "Daddy!"

How very peculiar, Doug thinks.

"Daddy!"

Doug starts awake with a grunt. He lies still, listening. He hears just the seep of the toilet. The thump and gurgle of the icemaker downstairs. He has nearly dropped off again when Jenny screams.

"Daddy!!"

Doug is running. Before he has flung back the spread, before he has rolled entirely out of bed, he is running. His legs churn in a panic. He bounces off the bureau. He barks against the doorjamb.

"Daddy!!"

Doug races blindly along the hallway. "I'm coming!"

He reaches Jenny's door. He feels about unsuccessfully for the light switch. He hears her. Whimpering. Doug sees in the darkened room, on Jenny's windowsill, the dim luminescence of the lizard's yellow eyes.

"He's in here!" she says. It is a low, quivering whisper.

"I see him. Stay put."

Doug finds the light switch and flips on the overhead globe. He eases across the room, his thumb and forefinger extended.

It allows him to pluck it from the sill. To carry it at arm's length down the darkened stairway and into the den. It remains placidly on the jar bottom while Doug searches for the lid. He scours the desktop. Examines the chair seat. He locates the thing against the baseboard halfway across the floor.

Doug threads the lid onto the jar rim and screws it down tight. He fetches a roll of packing tape from his desk drawer and runs a length of it about the rim.

"All right, smart guy," Doug says, peering into the jar, "now knock it off."

He sets the jar in his open satchel and heads back upstairs to find Jenny asleep again already, sprawled on her back. Doug switches off her light and stumbles down the hallway. He drops onto the mattress, drawing up the covers. He settles and moans. He dozes. He dreams.

He is running. His bare feet slap on the stones. His breath is shallow, labored. Ancient buildings rise on either side, blotting out the sky. Their windows are shuttered tight. The way is dusky. Close. Medieval.

Doug is in a desperate hurry. He cannot stop to rest. His route is complicated with turnings. He's uncertain of the way. Still he dashes, headlong and struggling for air.

He crosses a delicately arched bridge at a trot. The water beneath it is cloudy and still. It has a fetid, tidal reek. The sky is pink to the east with dawning. The way widens before a church. Narrows again. Doug is running.

He passes through an archway and into a massive square. It is floored in stone parquet with lengthy columned porticos to either side. Another church --domed and vaguely eastern-- dominates the far border. Doug dashes across the piazza. He must not be late.

To the south, the square opens onto water and headlands. Ahead to the east, Doug sees his destination. It is a palace. Pink marble. Massive portcullis windows. Lavish filigree. The square is vacant. The sky is brightening. Doug stops before the palace. Exhausted. Alone.

He hears dripping, the slap of liquid on stone. His cheek is wet. His forearm. A scarlet splatter. Blood. Doug lifts his gaze. Ten men hang by the neck from the palace windows above him. They are naked. They've been savagely battered and beaten, partially flayed. They are quite dead. As they swing slowly in the freshening sea air, their ropes creak and groan.

Torchlight seeps from the ornate entranceway to the palace. Doug hears a voice, the murmur of a priest in prayer.

"Quia peccavi nimis cogitatione, verbo et opere -- mea culpa, mea culpa, mea maxima culpa."

Doug approaches the entranceway. He passes into an inner courtyard, open to the sky. A grand marble staircase, adorned with colossal statues of Neptune and Mars, leads down from an upper balcony. A procession descends. It is lead by a priest in a cassock and miter. An acolyte --in a tunic with a pitch torch in hand-- lights his way.

"Omnes Sanctos, et vos, fratres, orare pro me ad Dominum Deum nostrum."

The priest is followed by a small, elderly man. He is bearded, sharp-featured, grim. A headsman, axe in hand, walks just behind him. The procession stops on the landing midway down the stairs.

Doug wishes to speak. He intends to announce that there are men, dead and bloodied, dangling from ropes just outside. He waves his arms. He claps his hands together.

He says instead, "Bless me, Father for I have sinned."

The priest and the acolyte ignore him. The headsman ignores him. Only the grim little man in the pointed cap and the rich scarlet cloak looks Doug's way as he lowers himself to kneel upon the landing.

The priest makes the sign of the cross. The boy with the torch makes the sign of the cross. Doug, politely, makes the sign of the cross.

"Siete condannato," the priest says, "al morte per i suoi delitti."

The priest nods to the headsman who raises his axe. The axe head is bronze. It is ornately etched, balefully sharp. The headsman swings it with a grunt.

93

The blade sunders flesh and sings against bone. The head of the grim little man separates cleanly from his shoulders. It tumbles across the landing and down the granite stairway, coming to rest at Doug's feet.

Doug decides he will run -- out the palace doorway, across the massive square, back again into the heart of the ancient city -- but he cannot move. He cannot turn and run. Doug can only speak again to the priest.

"Bless me, Father, for I have sinned."

The body of the grim, little man twitches on the landing. His head gushes blood at Doug's feet. From his mouth. From his eyes. From the stump of his neck. It flows along the seams between the stones. More blood than a grim, little man should hold. A river of it, coursing across the courtyard and draining through a chiseled stone grate.

It is the head of the grim, little man that speaks, in a bitter whisper-- low and blood-slurred. "Dieci da dieci. Per i suoi delitti."

They crawl through the grate by the dozens. They wriggle out through the chiseled slots. They are bathed in blood. Lizards. By the hundreds. The thousands. Doug hears the rasp of the their hides grating together as they dart and scamper. The rattle of their claws on stone.

They wash upon him like a tide, scuttling across his bare feet. Pouring into the piazza. He decides he must scream.

Doug jerks awake with a shout, bucking his head against the bedpost. He kicks the spread onto the floor. He blunders along the hallway and down the stairs, into the den.

He snatches the jar from his satchel. The lid is still snug, taped. Doug peers in at the creature on the jar bottom. Its malevolent yellow eyes glow.

23

Jack Proctor paces about his office. He speaks on his telephone through a headset. He sips at a mug of acrid, silty coffee. "No, no, no. It's nothing like that. He hit one in the gap and was going for third. You know Royce."

Proctor listens. He indulges in a bluff fraudulent laugh. "That's the truth of it, yes sir. He's prepped and ready to go. They'll cut on him tomorrow, and then he'll be laid up in rehab for a bit."

Proctor's office door swings open a crack and Pam sticks her head inside.

"I'll pass those good wishes along to Royce, and I'm sure he'll be giving you a call in a day or two."

Pam gives a little wave to catch Proctor's attention.

Proctor jerks off his headset. He raises his coffee mug. "Who the hell made this poison?"

"I did. Yesterday."

"Cappaccino grande. Send that dope from the copy pool."

"We've got company." Pam lowers her voice to a whisper. She jabs her thumb toward the outer office. "The majority leader."

Proctor fixes his lips into a broad smile. He takes a deep breath and charges into the outer office.

"Senator! What a pleasant surprise."

"Hello, Jack."

The majority leader shakes Jack Proctor's hand. He is nothing like Royce Tillman. He is distinguished and easily charming. He is cagey and discreet. He is blessed with a thick, tenacious crop of natural hair.

"Have you got a minute for me?"

"Of course, sir. Come right in."

Proctor ushers the majority leader into his office and shuts the door.

"How's Royce?"

"He's resigned to the surgery. Royce knows it was a fool accident. A little too much Maker's Mark and not enough water."

Jack Proctor looses one of his counterfeit snorts. The majority leader chuckles politely.

He lowers himself into a chair in front of Proctor's desk. He clasps his hands before him, intertwining his fingers.

"Playing a little softball out at the house?" he asks.

"Yes sir. With the grandkids."

"Funny. I've heard something else altogether."

"Oh?"

"A staffer of mine was on the Mall the other day."

Proctor lowers himself into his desk chair. He hopes he doesn't look as pasty as he feels.

"She claims she saw Royce, but he wasn't playing soft ball."

"Well, yes sir. He was having his photograph taken for the . . ."

The majority leader raises an open hand. It is quite enough of a gesture to interrupt Jack Proctor.

"After that, Jack."

"Well, then he came back here and . . ."

"I know for a fact it's not a knee. What it is, I can't say, but not a knee, now is it?"

Jack Proctor offers no response.

"How's it going to look for us if word gets out that Royce is . . . indisposed?" The majority leader rises from his seat. "He's been on point for a lot of years now. This might be for the best."

"He's going to be fine, sir. Believe me."

"I hope you're right, Jack, but we've got to think about the party. Sometimes you just have to move on. Have Royce call me when he's able." The majority leader smiles as he speaks. He pats Jack Proctor cordially on the back. He is richly blessed with what passes in politics for grace.

The majority leader dips a hand into his trouser pocket and strolls regally from the office. Jack Proctor drops into his desk chair with a groan. He swivels and pivots. He is short of breath. He feels dizzy and weak.

Proctor glances about at the photographs hanging on his walls. Royce and Delores at a state dinner. Royce and Delores in the rose garden with Reagan and Bush I. Royce and Delores in a fond embrace on the campaign trail. Royce and Delores holding hands in the Capitol rotunda. Cheney and Bush II sharing a laugh with the senior senator from Kentucky.

Proctor passes a moment in blind, frantic rage. He collects himself. He considers his situation. He calculates and charges out of his office to Pam's desk.

"See if you can get Delores Tillman in here."

"Today?"

"As soon as possible."

Proctor wheels about and starts toward his office door. He stops abruptly.

"Oh. What was that guy's name who danced at the Christmas party?"

"Which guy?"

"You know, the guy with the abs. I think he was Mexican or something."

"Fernando?"

"Yeah, Fernando. I want to talk to him too."

24

A grizzled old Muscovite digs through a trash barrel on Kalinskaya Prospekt. Soda bottles. Rotting blintzes. Meal worms. The tattered butt of a cigar. Hearing his name, he stops and stands.

He must go. South to the bank of the Moskva River. West to the Cathedral of the Annuniciation.

In the sanctuary, a Russian cleric chases a scarlet lizard with a broom. He is a comical sight in his cassock as he lumbers along the nave swatting desperately at the skink.

It scurries up onto a pew, and he catches it a solid blow with the broom straw. It is stilled and stunned. Upended. Dead perhaps.

As the cleric bends for a closer look, the lizard twitches. It parts its jaws. The stream of milky venom splatters against the cleric's forehead, dribbles down his cheeks. His eyes burn intolerably. His muscles tauten and contract. His breath won't come. His chest aches. He topples over onto the cold, stone floor in a tangle of vestments.

The grizzled old Muscovite passes slowly along the chancel aisle. He steps over the dead cleric and lays his hand onto the pew. The scarlet lizard crawls onto his palm. He covers it over. Lightly, gently. The smoke drifts in a gaudy plume toward the vaulted cathedral ceiling.

25

Beatrice sits at her cluttered desk talking on her telephone, which she has unearthed for the occasion. She consults a D.C. telephone directory as she speaks.

"Are you guys by any chance the Fighting Marauders? I mean like your football team? Your mascot?"

Amy, Beatrice's assistant, sticks her head through the door way..

"I see. Thanks."

"I've got Mr. Seville," Amy says, as Beatrice cradles the receiver.

"On two?"

Amy shakes her head. She points vaguely toward the outer corridor.

"He's here?"

Amy nods.

"He heard you on the phone. He knows you're in."

Beatrice throws up her hands. "Well, let him at me."

Amy steps into the hallway. She reappears in the company of Mr. Seville. He is spindly and angular. Nearly sixty. He looks like Orville Redenbacher's lost twin. He is rather showily dressed in a hounds-tooth blazer, a linen shirt, a silk ascot.

He strides in smiling confidently. Beatrice offers her hand.

"Mr. Seville, what a pleasant surprise."

He takes her hand in both of his. "Randolph, please."

Mr. Seville admires Beatrice. He holds securely to her fingers. "You're as lovely as I imagined."

"Oh . . . . Randolph. How very sweet."

Beatrice yanks her hand free with main force.
Randolph Seville approaches Beatrice's desk. He passes
a moment studying her desktop.

"What a blessing that you weren't injured . . . in the
fire."

Mr. Seville wanders about the room, drifting among
mounds of clutter. He plucks up the odd item that
attracts his gaze. Beatrice's salt-glazed teacup. A framed
photo of her parents. A hunk of quartzite. Beatrice's
red glass lizard.

"So, what brings you to town . . .Randolph?"

"If you'll recall, I told you I was coming. There was
talk of drinks. Perhaps dinner."

"Today?

"I suppose I should've called, but . . ." Randolph
Seville smiles and throws up his hands. "Voila!"

"Yes indeed. Voila."

"I'd be delighted to see where our Guarientos will
hang."

"Of course. We've set aside a wing for the show.
I'll walk you through."

"And then perhaps a cocktail?"

Beatrice considers the offer, nodding ever so slightly.
"Perhaps."

She gestures toward the door, but Randolph Seville
insists on following her from the office. She gets a whiff
of him as she passes. British Sterling and Altoids.
Beatrice can feel him watching her derriere. She pauses
at Amy's desk.

"Straight down that way," she says to Seville. "I'll be
right there."

Beatrice speaks in a whisper to Amy. "Come get me
in five minutes."

"For what?"

"Just come get me!"

Randolph Seville arrives at a junction in the
corridor. He looks left. Then right. He turns and calls

back to Beatrice, "I'm lost without you." He tosses his head as he laughs.

Mr. Seville insists upon resting his palm on the small of Beatrice's back. She cannot shrink and dodge sufficiently to keep him from squiring her through the gallery. He speaks of her stirring, pre-Raphaelite beauty. He mentions his waning affection for his wife. They move past the deconstructionists. The fauves. The impressionists. The romantic realists. The gentlemen's restroom. Beatrice feels the pressure of his clammy palm. It lays there on her back like a growth. Lumpish. Vaguely malignant. She checks her watch. She glances about for Amy.

"It's just that, these past few years, I've been ravenous for a change of scene."

"Oh," Beatrice hears herself say, "really?"

"Don't get me wrong, Cincinnati is vibrant and stimulating, but I'm wanderer at heart. Wouldn't it be marvelous if we could end up working together."

"Yes. Marvelous."

Beatrice checks her watch. She scans for Amy as they pass in among the Renaissance Italians. With light pressure, Mr. Seville steers Beatrice toward the finest of the Guarientos on display. It is a Veneto seascape, bright and vivid.

"How terribly charming," he says. "The reproductions hardly do it justice."

"We're fortunate to have it."

"I should say. It is nearly the equal of my canvases."

She pictures his murky, little still life. His indifferent landscape. She glances about desperately for Amy.

"Hi, Beatrice," she hears.

Howard. He approaches, smiling. Mr. Seville watches him with the gaze of a viper. Howard makes a remark. Beatrice sees his lips move, but she can't hear him for all the racket in her head. "What in the name of sweet Christ almighty did I do to deserve this!!?"

She can't conceive of what's preventing her from shouting it out loud. Instead, she grins blandly. Watching Randolph watch Howard. Watching Howard watch her.

"Ms. Malloy."

Beatrice turns to find Amy.

"There's a call for you. It's urgent."

"Thank you, Amy."

Beatrice physically detaches Mr. Seville's sweaty palm from the small of her back. "If you'll excuse me, gentlemen."

She takes a couple of steps across the creaky gallery floor. She pauses. "Oh, by the way. Randolph, this is Howard. Howard, Randolph."

They nod curtly, study each other uneasily. Randolph --with his ascot and patrician air. Howard -- with his toothy grin and clinging personal pathos.

Beatrice charges into the foyer, beneath the grand rotunda. She turns away from the administrative suite and toward the massive front entranceway, bathed in spring sunlight. She is out the door and down the grand front stairway in a flash. She crosses Constitution Avenue and heads north along 6th Street, nearly at a trot. Beatrice has no destination in mind, no earthly idea where she's going. She mutters to herself. She works her arms angrily, like a lunatic.

She hears, from just ahead on the walk, "Now what?"

It's Ted. He has found a parking spot on 6th. He has set his alarm with his key fob. His Saab has chirped and cooed. He has seen Beatrice stalking toward him in a simmering psychotic fury.

"Where the hell have you been!"

"I told you. I had to get a crown." Ted hooks a finger in the corner of his mouth and draws back his cheek to expose an artfully yellowed twelve-hundred-dollar molar.

"Look at me," Beatrice instructs him. She rotates fully on the sidewalk to allow Ted a full view. "Do I look desperate to you?"

"Talk to your Ted, sugar. What is it?"

"Seville's here."

"Oh, my." Ted drapes an arm around Beatrice's shoulder. He walks with her south along Sixth, back toward the gallery.

"The guy's been steering me around like a prom date." Beatrice draws a deep, sudden breath as she stops on the walk. "Have you got quarters?"

Beatrice is staring at a *USA Today* paper box by the curb.

Ted eyes the front page through the plexiglass window. The usual froth and piffle. A celebrity profile of a high-powered actress who loves her cats. A shrill account of a Tuskaloosa tornado. An up-with-America, full-color photograph -- the tidal-basin Japanese cherry trees in glorious bloom.

Ted hands over pocket change to Beatrice who shoves coins into the box and removes a paper. She points out to Ted a tease in the top right corner:

PC Wunderkind Slain
Bizarre Murder-Suicide Has Authorities Baffled

Beatrice opens the paper and reads of the death of a young London executive, Mr. Nathan Parker. It is, by *USA Today* standards, a full accounting. The considerable professional accomplishments of the victim. The odd confrontation in the office tower lobby. The cleanly severed arteries. The unknowable motives of the killer. His dementia. His wounds. His Italian.

Ted reads over Beatrice's shoulder. "Now that's pretty weird," he says.

Beatrice's eyes stray to a small item at the bottom of the page. Beneath the obituary for a child star of the twenties. Beside brief notice of the death by drowning of the popular mayor of Carson City. It is a scant paragraph. Sketchy information from a wire service report. A young Canadian tourist has been murdered in the streets of Alexandria, Egypt. Stabbed.

The available information is contradictory and incomplete. The killer has escaped detection. The killer has been captured and has confessed. The killer has taken his own life as well.

"Oh my God." Beatrice says in a breathy whisper. "Two more."

"Two more what?"

She folds the paper shut and wanders south along the street. Ted follows. They cross Constitution, veer around the National Gallery building, and continue onto the Mall. "We're back on lizards again, aren't we?"

Beatrice drops onto a vacant bench. Ted settles in beside her. "So this is the way the world ends, not with a bang but a geezer?"

"I need to find that lizard. Tillman's lizard. If Tillman gets it, somebody dies. Somebody young. Innocent probably."

"In this town!?"

"Help me out. You saw that school bus."

"Come on, Beety. We don't want to be messing around with a six-hundred-year-old curse."

"Help me! The bus!"

"Okay, okay. The Raging Vikings. . ?"

"The Fighting Marauders," Beatrice says sternly.

"And we've ruled out Aaron Burr?"

Beatrice cuts a sharp sidelong glance.

"John Quincy Adams? Paul Revere? Abe Lincoln? Henry Kissinger?"

"Help. Me."

"Thomas Dewey? Ben Franklin? Horace Greeley? Nathan Hale? Patrick Henry? Snidely Whiplash? . . . "

"Wait, wait, wait."

"Snidely Whiplash?"

"Patrick Henry."

Beatrice tries to picture the bus. Turning off of Constitution. Rolling out of sight.

"That's it! Patrick Henry. The Fighting Marauders. Patrick Henry High."

Beatrice jumps to her feet and kisses Ted on the top of the head.. She rushes across the lawn toward the back entrance to the National Gallery. By the time Ted rises from the bench, she is trotting across the to gallery landing.

An elderly man approaches along the gravel walk. He moves haltingly, with the aid of a cane. His features are fixed in a permanent scowl. He scowls left, toward the Air and Space Museum. He scowls at a gray squirrel crossing his path. He lifts his head and scowls at Ted.

Ted ruminates still upon curses and lizards. Old men killing young men. Death by the blade. Messy, he suspects. Painful.

Ted resolves to be scrupulously kind to his elders from here on out. Simply as a preventative and a precaution. He decides to begin with the gentleman at hand.

Ted smiles sweetly. "Hello," he says.

26

Jack Proctor draws a deep, settling breath. He
swings open his office door. He smiles. "Delores, how
good of you to come."

"Why thank you, Jack. You remember Lewis."

Naturally Jack remembers Lewis. Pale intern.
Cheap blazer. Goofy smile. But the creature he extends
his hand to is clad entirely in Armani. His hair is shorn
stylishly close. Sun has colored his face becomingly.

Delores Tillman has remanufactured Lewis in the
course of two days. Lewis steps forward to take Jack's
hand. He fails to look Proctor squarely in the eye.

"Hello, sir," he says in a low mumble.

Lewis is ashamed. He has allowed himself to be
seduced by Mrs. Royce Tillman. He feels that he has
tempted her unduly. That he has served with his
muscular physique and his remarkable good looks to stir
her appetites and passions. He feels vaguely unpatriotic.

"So, I've come running. What's up, Jack?"

"Perhaps we could talk in here."

He takes Delores Tillman lightly by the elbow and
guides her toward his office door. She enters. Proctor
follows and shuts the door, leaving Lewis outside.

"Please sit." He directs her to a club chair in the
corner of his office. Proctor leans against his desk.

"Have you stopped in to see Royce?" Proctor asks.

"Goodness no. How is the poor boy's knee?"

"It's about the same."

"Pity."

"The doctors say it might not get any better."

"No!"

Proctor nods.

"Such a tragedy," Delores says. "And Royce used to
be so . . . agile."

"It's starting to look like he'll have to give up his
seat."

Delores smiles. "Why should he? What's one more invalid in the Senate, more or less?"

"The majority leader stopped by. They smell blood in the water."

"Oh?"

"They want him to resign so they can replace him. I hear they've got their hearts set on the lieutenant governor."

"That hayseed!?"

Jack nods. "Of course, I'll be needing your limo. And the keys to the co-op."

"I beg your pardon!"

"Royce ran the leases through the office. He didn't tell you?"

Stunned, Delores Tillman can only shake her head.

"There'll be a little messiness with the estate as well, but we can probably work that out."

Jack Proctor pauses dramatically. He glances forlornly out his office window. "At least, I hope so."

"You hope so!?"

Proctor shrugs. "You know Royce. Cut a corner, save a buck."

Delores Tillman rises from her chair and nervously crosses the breadth of the office and back.

"There's nothing we can do? I mean, maybe Royce'll get better. Let's not be hasty here."

"To tell you the truth, Delores, we simply don't have a lot of options." Jack Proctor indulges in meditative silence. "There's one, but it's . . . I'm reluctant to even bring it up."

"What!? What is it!?"

"You could take over for Royce."

"What do you mean? Take over how?"

Proctor circles his desk and pauses in a back corner of his office where the stars and stripes and the flag of Kentucky hang limply on wooden masts.

"You could serve in Royce's place. Run for his seat once he's deemed unfit. I'm sure the sympathy vote alone will see you through."

"Me? A senator?"

Proctor nods.

"Jack, darling, you know I've no taste for politics."

"If I may, Delores, you seem to like the trappings well enough. And unless you want to pack up and move back to Lexington . . . ."

Delores Tillman wanders the office in a reverie.

"Senator Delores Tillman. I confess I do rather like the sound of that."

Jack smiles.

"And stop and think for a minute, Delores. The power. The glamour. It shifts from him to you. You'll travel the world on the government's dime. Meet anybody you want. Do pretty much whatever you please."

"And the . . . business of the nation?"

"You make a few speeches. Meet and greet. There's nothing to it. I'll take care of everything else."

Delores Tillman sinks into the club chair. She considers the prospect, smiling slightly.

"I suppose we should think of Royce," she says. "His legacy, I mean."

"Of course."

"Could I have my own staff?"

"Certainly."

"Perhaps a . . .traveling secretary. It's a big, cold world out there, Jack."

"Funny you should ask."

Jack Proctor hits his intercom button. "Pam."

"Yes sir?"

"Send him in."

The office door swings opens almost immediately. A young man enters. He is muscular. Swarthy. Latin.

"This is Fernando, Delores. I believe you two met at the Christmas party."

Delores Tillman's eyes brighten at the sight of Fernando. She appears to remember him quite well.

"How lovely to see you again," Delores says as she lays a hand to Fernando's sinewy forearm.

"Afternoon, ma'm."

"Fernando here takes dictation, don't you?"

Fernando -- exhaustively prepped and instructed, handsomely paid -- smiles broadly and nods.

"Maybe you'd like to try him out. He's free for the afternoon. Aren't you Fernando?"

"Yes sir, quite free."

Delores Tillman lightly runs her hand along Fernando's sleeve.

"Jack, Jack, Jack. Aren't you the perfect scoundrel."

Delores stands and offers her fingers to Jack. She hooks her arm through Fernando's.

"Come, darling. Let's see what you can do."

Delores pauses by the door. She turns back toward Jack.

"You'll explain things to Lewis, won't you? He's a dear boy, but that silly grin." She shakes her head.

"I'll talk to him. You kids have fun."

Delores wiggles her fingers at Proctor.

"Ta ta."

"Ciao," Proctor says.

He waves, knuckles out, in the Italian fashion.

27

Beatrice rarely drives these days. What with the bus. The Metro. Her dull existence. The constitutional frailties of her Opal Kadet.

She crosses the Potomac on the Francis Scott Key Bridge and takes the Lee Highway west toward Falls Church. Her passenger seat is freighted with books and newspapers. Her proof.

She has a volume of Venetian history. A National Gallery catalog. *Il Gazzettino*. *USA Today*. A fresh edition of *The London Times*.

Beatrice's oil light blinks on. Her temperature needle eases steadily toward the peg. Her tires are bald and cracked about the sidewalls. She notices that her inspection sticker is eight months out of date. The engine lugs and sputters.

"Come on, baby." The motor revives and smoothes out. Beatrice rubs her palm gently along the dashboard, her preferred form of auto maintenance. "That's a girl."

To find Patrick Henry High School, she only has to ask directions twice. It's nearly five o'clock by the time she pulls into the schoolhouse lot. Her engine diesels as she switches it off. She hears anti-freeze simmering in her radiator.

Beatrice hurries up the front steps and into the high school proper. In the administrative office, the school secretary, Mrs. Kiley, is tidying up her desk and preparing to leave for the day.

As Beatrice enters, Mrs. Kiley eyes her over her spectacles.

"May we help you?"

"I'm looking for a little girl."

"Which little girl."

"I'm not entirely sure."

"And who are you exactly?"

Beatrice digs through her purse. She scrapes up from the bottom a trio of business cards. She hands Mrs. Kiley the one that's least dinged and damaged.

"Beatrice Malloy. I'm with the National Gallery of Art. This little girl was on the Mall a couple of days ago. She got onto one of your buses. I'm guessing her class was visiting the Natural History Museum."

Mrs. Kiley exhales wearily. "What's she done?"

"Nothing. Not a thing. I just think she might have found a lizard on the Mall. A fairly exotic one, and I wanted to talk to her about it."

Janice, in her topcoat and with her satchel in hand, steps in from the hallway for a final check of her box.

"There was a man with her," Beatrice adds. "A teacher, I guess. Dark hair. Six feet."

Mrs. Kiley is studying the business card again. "Now what's this about a lizard?"

"The little girl found it. I guess she took it home."

Mrs. Kiley looks from the business card to Beatrice. She studies her indelicately for a moment. "You're an art historian?"

"Well, yes, but . . ."

"Was it a red lizard?"

Janice stands before the mail cubbies looking at Beatrice. Severe hair. Bland, baggy clothes. Clunky shoes. Potential, though. And female.

"Yes."

"Were you on the Mall the other day?"

"Yes! Have you seen it!? Do you know where it is!?"

"I might."

Doug has neglected to thaw the London broil he intended to roast for dinner. He stands in the middle of the kitchen floor holding the frozen chunk of meat in hand, weighing his options when he hears the door chime.

"Jenny."

Nothing. Jenny is sprawled on her bed with a spiral notebook. She performs tedious long division. She listens to music through her earphones.

"Jenny!"

The door chime sounds again. Doug leaves the kitchen for the dining room, his frozen hunk of meat in hand. He crosses into the foyer and draws open the door.

"Hi. Doug Gunther?" Beatrice stands with her books and newspapers under her arm. She smiles at Doug. At his frozen roast. Her ancient Opal Kadet sits chugging in his driveway. Puffs of blue smoke escape from the exhaust pipe.

"Aren't you the woman from the Mall?"

"Yeah. Beatrice Malloy. Hi."

He smiles. He wears jeans. A ratty Georgetown sweatshirt. Dilapidating canvas sneakers. He is slightly cuter than she remembers. His smile sweeter. His eyes kinder.

"Your friend Janice sent me. She thought it would be all right."

"Yeah, of course. It's fine."

"I think we need to talk."

"Talk, right. Maybe you want to shut off your car."

Beatrice shows Doug the ignition key in her free hand. "I'm told it's the timing." The Kadet gives a final, combustive burp and falls silent.

"May I?" Beatrice steps past Doug and into the foyer. "I'm here about a lizard. Janice says you have him." Beatrice digs out a business card and offers it to Doug.

"Is he yours?"

"Not exactly. This is sort of complicated."

112

Beatrice moves to place her books and newspapers on a side table in the front foyer. Locks of her hair have slipped from her beret. She unclasps the thing, shakes her head, and looses her hair to fall freely about her shoulders.

The transformation is so complete as to be stunning. What was stern and forbidding about her has suddenly melted away. She is lovely, in spite of the baggy frock. Brown, Doug notices. In spite of the clunky shoes. He suspected as much on the Mall.

"This is one very unusual lizard," she says.

"You'll get no argument from me. But how do you know about him?"

Beatrice reaches into her pocket and pulls out an item bundled in tissue. She carefully unwraps it. Displays it on her palm. "A good likeness?"

"Where on earth did you get that?" Doug plucks up the glass lizard gently between his fingers. He considers it closely. "I looked through every book I could find," he says. "There is no red skink. Not anywhere."

"It was my mother's. She's from Murano."

"Where?"

"The outer lagoon. Venice."

Doug lifts his eyes from the glass lizard. "Italy?"

Beatrice nods, and Doug steps a little numbly into the dining room. He draws out a chair and sits. He settles the glass lizard before him on the tabletop. Beatrice takes up her books and papers from the side table and joins Doug.

"Listen, I know what I'm about to say is going to sound crazy, but I think your red lizard is no normal creature. I think it's part of a . . . vendetta. It was meant for Senator Royce Tillman. He's been . . . selected.

"The guy on the mall? With the rug?"

Beatrice nods.

113

"Selected for what?"

"To kill. And probably to die."

"Senator Royce Tillman. Kentucky, right?"

Beatrice nods.

"So when you say vendetta, you mean . . .?"

"A curse," Beatrice concedes. "Believe me, I know how this sounds" She sorts through her papers. She points out the articles to Doug. "But there are two dead in London. In Venice. In Egypt. And God knows where else. And then there's Tillman."

"What happened to him anyway? Is he any better? I read that stuff about his knee."

"I went to see him in the hospital. He speaks nothing but Italian now. He wants his 'lucertola'. His 'condottiero'. His lizard. His guide."

"Odd."

"It gets odder. These killings are all essentially the same, like rituals. Identical wounds. Apparently, the same words as well. Per I suoi delitti. Also Italian. It means. . ."

"For you crimes."

"Ah, parla l'Italiano?"

Doug fishes from his trouser pocket a folded sheet of notepaper with a scrap of prose he'd remembered from his dream, a phrase he'd translated by the language arts teacher at school. Per I suoi delitti.

"No," he says, a little stunned. "Not a word."

28

As is her custom, Janice has sought Hank's advice in order to ignore it.

"So you don't think I should call him?" Janice says. She has their kitchen wall phone receiver in hand.

"Didn't I just say that?"

"But what if he needs to talk to me?"

"He can't call out from his house!? Leave the poor man alone. If he wants a girlfriend, he can find one himself."

"No he can't."

Hank groans.

"I'm going to call him," Janice says. "I'm going to call him right now."

Hank shakes his head and wanders out of the kitchen. Janice punches in Doug's number on the phone.

Jenny, in between songs and sick of long division, takes up the receiver on the first ring.

"Gunther residence. Hey."

Jenny rolls onto her back. She chews on the phone cord.

"What woman?"

Jenny draws the receiver away from her ear. She hears them now.

"Yeah, she is here. Let me go see. I'll call you back."

Jenny cradles the receiver and rolls out of bed.

Downstairs in the den, Doug and Beatrice stand side-by-side peering into the pickle jar.

"What a color! And those eyes!

"Yeah, he's an odd one."

The red skink sprawls calmly on the jar bottom eyeing them back. Beatrice considers the strip of packing tape around the lid. "What's this?"

"He's a little too resourceful," Doug says. "So what's the story with this guy?"

"Best guess? La sangue lucertola. A blood lizard. Bigfoot Venetian style. Let me show you something."

Carrying the jar, Beatrice leads Doug out of the den and the back into the dining room. Jenny is pressed against the stairwell wall, lurking. Doug and Beatrice fail to notice her as they pass. She eases down to the next to last tread with quiet stealth and lingers just out of sight.

Beatrice sets the jar on the table. She takes up the National Gallery catalog and opens it to a reproduction of the Veronese canvas. Falieri on the Molo. The uplifted pikes. The kneeling clerics. The richly embroidered robe, swarming with needlework lizards. It all looks chillingly familiar to Doug.

"What do you know about Venice?" Beatrice asks him.

"Not much. Streets full of water . . ." Doug trails off. Shrugs.

"Actually, I mean ancient Venice. The queen of the Adriatic. La Serenissima -- the most serene republic."

"Hardly anything."

Doug lowers himself into a chair. He runs his finger over Falieri's embroidered cloak.

"She was once a world power. Venice was the seat of empire. The gateway to the east."

Beatrice opens her volume of Venetian history and shows Doug an etching of the lagoon and the molo in the days of the republic. Ships crowd the harbor. The piazza teems with merchants.

"Venetians were seafarers, traders, mercenaries. They were a formidable people. Ruthless. Vengeful. And, for Italians anyway, unbelievably scrupulous and precise. Even the city itself, according to Venetian lore, was founded in 421 a.d. at precisely twelve noon on the

116

twenty-fifth of March. About a thousand years later, Marino Falieri was executed on the twenty-fifth of March." Beatrice indicates the regal figure in the Veronese painting.

"He got his head lopped off, didn't he?" Doug says. "In a courtyard. On the palace stairs. His buddies got strung up from the windows. Am I right?"

Beatrice nods. "How do you know that?"

Doug smiles. "I don't really sleep like I used to."

Jenny edges down the stairwell. She steals a peek at Beatrice around the corner. Pretty hair. Dull, brown dress. Dougie's color.

"Marino Falieri was a pretty odd bird," Beatrice says. "Sour, paranoid, and, late in his life, fairly deep into the black arts."

"Witchcraft?"

"Negromanzia. More like sorcery. A perversion of science. Do you know why he was beheaded?"

Doug shakes his head.

"He plotted to kill all the young male aristocrats in Venice."

"Why?"

"He was old. Tired. His wife was young, ravishing, and hungry for . . .affection. It seems she'd take it wherever she found it. A number of the young bucks in the city happily accommodated her. Falieri resented them for it."

"Wouldn't it have been a lot easier just to kill his wife?"

"Apparently he loved her. Anyway, he was the king, and he had some graybeards eager to help him. Ten of them counting Falieri. It probably seemed like a good idea at the time. And I don't suppose, in the thirteen hundreds, there were all that many young men in Venice anyway. Why not polish them off?"

"But Falieri and his pals got found out, right?"

Beatrice nods.

"And killed off."

117

Beatrice nods.

"So what's all of this got to do with him?"   Doug points toward the lizard in his jar on the table.

Beatrice takes up the glass lizard from the tabletop. "When my mother was a child, these things were common in the Veneto. Sangue Lucertole. Blood lizards. The glass blowers used to make them by the thousands. They were thought to be magic. Charmed." She looks toward the scarlet skink in the jar. "I guess what I'm trying to tell you is that maybe they actually are."

Beatrice lays out before Doug her web printouts from the archives of *Il Gazzettino*.

"Falieri's Curse. Dieci da dieci. Ten by ten. Ten murders every ten years. Ten suicides. Maybe it's not a fable after all."

"So you think Falieri has somehow reached from beyond the grave? That's what you're telling me?"

"Listen, I know you don't know me from Adam, but I'm not crazy. I think Oswald shot Kennedy and it was a weather balloon in Roswell. This is different."

Doug gazes past Beatrice toward the wall behind her where a picture hangs. It is a portrait of his late wife. Robust. Vibrant. Vigorously alive.

"Believe me, I realize this all sounds awfully far-fetched, but I just don't . . .can't . . ." Beatrice trails off, at a loss for the right words, a proper rational reassurance.

Doug helps her out. "Sometimes," he says, shifting his gaze from the photo to Beatrice, "the dead just won't stay buried."

Doug catches brief sight of Jenny, peeking around the wall by the stairwell. "What are you doing?"

Caught, Jenny steps into the foyer.

"This is Jenny. I thought she'd outgrown her Boo Radley phase."

"Daddy!"

"This is Miss Malloy."

"Can you cook?"

118

"Jenny!"

"'Cause I'm hungry, and he burns everything."

Doug grins helplessly at Beatrice.

29

He has been waiting for a starlet. In his ratty Dodge van with his telephoto lens. He hoped for a shot of her jogging. A shot of her carrying her golden-haired toddler. A candid view of her looking, perhaps, a trifle doughy and unglamorous.

She is to testify before congress in her capacity as a celebrated movie star with unqualified opinions. She will be ready for the cameras on the Hill. He wants her wholly unprepared. Unflatteringly candid. It is his stock and trade.

But nothing, and all day he's been sitting. Waiting. Smoking. He is packing away his lenses as they emerge from the Ritz-Carlton lobby. He recognizes the woman from the television news. Her little chat outside the hospital. The senator's wife.

She is with a swarthy young man. She clutches his arm in a way that is not chaste and motherly. As they approach their limo at the curb, she swabs the young man's ear canal with her tongue.

The motor drive hums. The shutter mechanism chatters. The photographer starts his van. On a whim, he follows them east to Dupont Circle, and then south along New Hampsire and out of town.

They travel to a lovely estate near Middleburg. A fine Georgian house. Spectacular grounds. Thousands of boxwoods -- massive and sourly aromatic.

The photographer lurks in the shrubbery. He has an open view of the hot tub across the lawn. The patio lights are on. The senator's wife and her young friend relax, naked, in the swirling, steaming water. They sip champagne. They chat. They embrace and kiss.

Delores Tillman sets her champagne flute aside and rolls onto Fernando's lap, mounting him. She rocks slowly, her head flung back.

Such a lovely night for romance. The moon. The stars. The crickets in the shrubbery. Click click click click click click click.

30

It is actual meat sauce with flavor and spices. It is served on linguine that Beatrice has failed to scorch and overcook. She has made an edible salad out of their iceberg lettuce. She has sipped Doug's hearty burgundy without complaint.

"This is great!" Jenny smiles broadly at Beatrice. "Isn't it, Daddy?"

"Yeah. Really good."

Jenny eats another forkful. She chews it with showy, advertising savor. "You have pretty hair. Doesn't she daddy?"

"Yes, very pretty."

"Do you have a boyfriend?"

"Jenny!" Doug treats Jenny to his all-purpose, head-of-household glare. She ignores him. "I mean, like, serious?"

Doug cuts a glance Beatrice's way, gauging her reaction.

"Not at the moment."

"Did you hear that, Dougie?"

"I will put you in the crawl space with the spiders. Leave Miss Malloy alone."

"Beatrice, please."

"Do you like my dad?"

"Jenny!! Enough!" Doug smiles helplessly at Beatrice.

"I don't know. Do you like him?"

"He's all right." Beatrice and Jenny consider Doug. "He can't dress himself because he's colorblind. And he burns everything he cooks. But he's okay."

122

"Are there military schools for girls?" Doug asks Beatrice.

In its jar on the counter top, the scarlet lizard makes a quick scuttling circuit. Its feet scratch against the jar lid. Jenny turns to watch it from the table.

"I thought you were getting rid of him, Daddy."

"Tomorrow," Doug says. "I've got a friend at the zoo," he tells Beatrice. "A snake guy. He can at least tell us what it's not."

"Mind if I tag along?"

"Around five okay?"

"Fine."

"I'll swing by and pick you up."

Beatrice reaches for the pickle jar to take a closer look at the lizard. "But you're not going to leave him there, right? Because, as strange as this sounds, I'm thinking this lizard might be Tillman's only chance."

"That senator?" Jenny asks.

"Yeah. He's . .uh . . sick," Beatrice says, glancing at Doug.

"Sick with what?"

"Hard to say," Doug tells Jenny.

"In the hospital?"

Beatrice nods. "GWU. I saw him. He's pretty bad off."

"And that skink can cure him?" Jenny asks.

"Well," Beatrice says, glancing at Doug. "We don't really know for sure."

Beatrice peers into the jar. She taps with her fingernail on the glass.

"No!" Doug and Jenny shout together.

The gullet distends. The jaws hinge open. They clap their hands to their ears.

Even an hour later, Beatrice is still a little shaken and embarassed. She hadn't intended to leap onto her chairseat. She hardly meant to wail and shriek. She sits at the table sipping from a cup of hot tea as Doug washes the dinner dishes.

From a safe distance and with no quick movements, Beatrice peers again into the jar. The scarlet lizard, curled placidly on the jar bottom, considers her back.

"Better?" Doug asks, glancing toward Beatrice over his shoulder. She nods sheepishly. Still shaken. Still a little embarrassed.

"I've never heard anything quite like that."

"Yeah. He's got some lungs on him."

Doug dries his hands. He steps to the refrigerator. Dessert?" He opens the refrigerator door and peers inside.

"I think there's pound cake in here somewhere."

"No, thanks. I'd better be going."

"Let's count on tomorrow around five?"

Beatrice nods. "Sounds good."

They step together into the dining room. Beatrice gathers up her books and papers. Doug continues to the stairwell.

"Jenny! Come say goodbye to Beatrice."

In her bedroom upstairs, Jenny sits at her desk. She consults her laminated D.C. streetmap. Her handy pocket-sized Metrorail guide. She holds in her hand a snapshot of her mother. It's one she keeps hidden away in a drawer.

In the photo, Gail sits on the edge of her hospital bed in a housecoat. She is drawn and jaundiced. Pallid and failing. Infuriatingly incurable.

Jenny stands the snapshot against a book on her desktop before her. For resolve. "I'm coming."

She runs downstairs. She flings herself at Beatrice. Embraces her. Even Jenny is a little surprised.

"Bye."

"Bye yourself."

Jenny bolts back upstairs. She scampers into her bedroom and shuts her door.

Doug walks Beatrice to her Kadet. It sits beside his Camry in the drive in a pool of iridescent anti-freeze. The left rear tire, Doug notices, has gone entirely flat. Beatrice, oblivious, opens the driver's door and slips in under the wheel.

"You've been very understanding. Thank you."

"Yeah, sure."

Doug looks from the puddled coolant to the flat rear tire. Beatrice turns her key. Her engine chugs to life. Doug reaches in and switches it off.

31

In her bedroom, Jenny sits at her desk. The pickle jar rests on the desktop before her. Jenny peers in at the scarlet lizard. It watches her from the jar bottom. It sits utterly still, its tail curled beneath its trunk. The scarlet lizard flicks its tongue with a quick, chilling rasp.

Jenny swallows hard, firming her resolve. She peels the packing tape from around the jar rim. She unscrews the lid. The creature permits her to reach in and close it round with her fingers. It allows her to lift it out.

The scarlet lizard lounges on Jenny's palm. It doesn't twitch or dart. It doesn't offer to hiss. Jenny strokes the lizard lightly along its back with her finger.

Doug slows to a stop in Georgetown before Beatrice's building. He eases to the curb.

"I really appreciate this. I'll call for a tow in the morning."

Beatrice swings open her door.

"So I guess I'll see you tomorrow."

Without planning to, Doug opens his door as well. He climbs out of the car.

"I'll walk you up."

"You don't need to do that."

"I don't mind."

Doug is twitchy and anxious. Not Barbara twitchy, but something else altogether. Agreeably nervous. Edgy and sweaty-palmed like a kid.

Beatrice lets herself into the building, and Doug follows her up the stairs to her apartment door. She throws back the bolt.

"Do you want to come in?"

"Maybe just for a second."

His voice sounds distant to him and annoyingly high-pitched.

Gus is waiting at the door as they enter. He yowls and mews. He rubs generous tufts of cat hair onto Doug's trousers. Doug gazes wide-eyed around the cluttered front room. "Wow!" he says without meaning to have said it.

"What?"

"You're . . . . messy." He says it with delight. Glee even. "Gail, my wife, she was a slob too."

Sensing the possible offense, Doug lays a hand to Beatrice's arm. "I'm sorry. I know it's not a personal failing. It's a philosophy. That's what Gail always said."

"So I'm just . . ."

"Deeply, deeply philosophical."

Doug feels himself grinning. Broadly. Foolishly. He decides he will shake Beatrice's hand. He informs himself that that is all he will do. He doesn't want to drive this one off.

"Well, I guess I'm glad we've had this little visit," Beatrice says. "Can I offer you something? Coffee?"

"No, thanks. I've got to get back." Doug turns toward the door. Beatrice draws it open for him.

"Thanks again."

"My pleasure."

Doug can't swallow. He is desperate to think of something crisp and jolly to say before he steps into the hallway. At least something uninsulting and polite. Doug pinches a bit of Beatrice's dress between his fingers.

"This is a pretty shade of brown," he tells her.

In fact, it is a pretty shade of brown.

32

In Mozambique, the Boer guide of a hunting party takes his morning bath in the Zambezi river. He sits naked in a shallow eddy with a battered tin mug of tea and a sliver of soap.

He has seen it coming on the sluggish current. He spied it as it washed from the bend. As he sips his Earl Grey and lathers his torso, he watches it bob and drift.

It is black and slick with water. Not a log or a crocodile as he first suspected. Instead a carcass, bloated and buoyant. It drifts toward him. It enters his eddy and circulates slowly shoreward.

He grabs a leg and runs it aground onto a silty bar. It is a man. Black. Bony. Tattooed. Toothless. Ancient. He has swollen in the sun. He has been gnawed on in the river. The hilt of knife protrudes from his chest. Between his ribs. Beside his sternum.

He is smiling.

33

Jenny is unusually chatty on the way to school. She speaks to Doug at length about her plans and obligations for the day. A test in spelling. A book report. Lunch with Rebecca and Dawn. Majorette tryouts after school.

"Since when do you want to be a majorette?"

"Dawn's trying out. We're just going to watch her."

"Which one's Dawn."

"Blue hair."

"Right."

Doug pulls into the loop before Jenny's school. He rolls to a stop before the entranceway. Without prompting, Jenny leans over and kisses him on the cheek.

"Bye, daddy."

"Have a good day, sweetie. Try to be home by four, okay?"

Jenny nods.

"Got your key?"

Jenny slaps at the back pocket of her book bag. But gently. Carefully. "Right here."

She climbs from the car and waves to Doug from the sidewalk. He eases out of the loop toward the street. Doug's leather satchel rests beside him on the seat. Just beyond it sits the brown paper sack --its neck rolled tightly shut-- that Jenny has thoughtfully packed with the lizard jar for Doug and Beatrice's trip to the zoo.

Jenny watches her father turn onto the roadway and accelerate out of sight.

When he finds her office empty, Ted quite naturally looks for Beatrice in with the Venetians. Instead, he sees only a pair of docents. Two women. Junior league types. They stand before a Bellini seascape. They appear to be admiring the frame.

Just by chance, as he's returning through the galleries, Ted spies a woman parked before a Degas. An interior. Dark and thickly varnished. A couple in repose. They gaze dreamily at each other.

The woman looks familiar to Ted. Beautiful flowing hair. A handsome tailored suit in a delicate mauve. Stunning heels. He has already looked away before he realizes who she is.

"Oh. My. God!" Ted says in an urgent whisper. "Beety!?"

Ted crosses to her at a trot. He lays his hands to his cheeks and drops his mouth open in one of his stagy demonstrations of utter disbelief.

"Get it out of your system," Beatrice snarls.

"Darling, you're transformed!" Ted circles Beatrice. He looks her up and down. "You've got . . .like . .legs and hips and cleavage. Look at this." Ted pinches up a bit of Beatrice's dress fabric between his fingers. "It's a color!"

"That'll do."

Beatrice sets out across the gallery toward the rotunda and the administrative suite beyond. Ted runs to catch up. "So what happened? And please don't tell me you're just going to the gynecologist."

Beatrice stops and turns toward Ted. She smiles. She can't seem to keep from smiling.

"I found him," she says.

"Lucertole?"

"Doug."

"That's a funny name for a lizard."

"The guy. Remember? From the mall?"

"The Fighting Marauder."

Beatrice nods. "He's coming by this afternoon with the lizard. His daughter caught it over by the skating rink and took it home. We're going to carry it to a friend of his at the zoo. Some herpetologist."

So Doug's behind this?" Ted gestures to indicate Beatrice's dress, her flowing hair, her general loveliness.

Beatrice shrugs by way of admission.

"Brought together by a six-hundred-year-old curse," Ted says. "Talk about meeting cute."

34

Pam swings open Jack Proctor's office door a crack and stick her head inside.

"A Mr. Vaughn is here to see you."

"Conner?"

"Yes sir."

Proctor rises from his desk. He crosses to his office door and swings it open. Conner Vaughn, of the Rhode Island Vaughns, stands beside Pam's desk.

He smiles warmly at Proctor. He offers his hand. In the other he holds a large envelope. "Jack. Good to see you. I hope you've got a minute."

"Yeah, sure. Come on in."

Jack Proctor claps Conner Vaughn on the back as he ushers him into his office. They detest each other, but always politely and with phony cordiality. They work on opposite sides of the aisle. Their politics and sensibilities are diametrically opposed.

Conner Vaughn comes from old, Wasp money and a family history of liberal causes. He works as the chief of staff for the senior senator from New York. He is haughty and dismissive. A hopeless bleeding-heart. Jack Proctor can barely stand the sight of him.

"Please. Sit."

Jack shows Conner Vaughn to the chair opposite his desk. He hates Vaughn's navy blazer with its scarlet and gold heraldic crest on the breast pocket. His loafers and khakis. His signet ring. His casually combed walnut hair.

"How's Mitsy?" Jack asks as her lowers himself into his desk chair.

"Good, good. Thanks for asking. How's Royce? I hear he had a bit of a spell."

132

"Nothing serious. He tore up a knee."

"So you're still going with that?" Conner Vaughn smiles slyly. "Word travels, you know?"

Jack says nothing for a moment. "What can I do for you, Conner?"

"I hate to be the bearer of bad tidings, Jack, but these came my way this morning, and I thought you'd want to see them." Conner Vaughn tosses the envelope onto Proctor's desk.

"You know Phil Bowen, don't you? At the *Post?*"

Jack Proctor nods as he works open the envelope flap.

"He said these were on offer from some free-lance shutterbug. I believe the *Daily News* snatched them up. *Hard Copy* as well."

Jack Proctor draws from the envelope a half dozen eight by ten glossies in glorious color. They are a bit grainy but clear enough to reveal Delores Tillman and young, strapping Fernando cavorting in a hot tub.

"Just as nature intended, huh Jack?"

Proctor resists the temptation to leap across his desk and strangle Conner Vaughn. He strains to maintain a serene expression. He won't give Vaughn the satisfaction of looking shocked and distressed.

"I guess it never rains but it pours," Conner Vaughn adds as he stands. "Sorry, old boy, but I thought you might want a heads up. You know, family values and all that. Could be a problem with the voters back home. Damned liberal media." Conner Vaughn chuckles.

Jack Proctor only glares at him by way of response.

"I guess I'll show myself out."

Conner Vaughn fairly skips from the office. Proctor returns his attention to the photographs. They are unobscured and utterly unambiguous. They are damning and indefensible. Proctor groans and lays his head on his desk.

A lunatic senator in the hospital speaking exclusively Italian. The lunatic senator's wife naked on the lap of a part-time underwear model and party favor. Proctor groans again. He reaches for the bottom pull and yanks open a drawer. Proctor takes from it a bottle of scotch. Johnny Walker. Black. Proctor dumps the dregs of his coffee into the begonia on his desk. He pours himself a half mug of scotch and drains it. He pours himself another.

"Cheers," he says as he raises his mug toward his wall of photos. Delores and Royce, devoted power couple.

Proctor pours off his dram and tilts the bottle yet again.

35

Jenny sits at her school desk watching the clock on the wall above the door. A quarter hour to go. Her book bag rests on her lap. She peers yet again into the unzipped opening. He sprawls quietly on his jar bottom. From the murky depths of her knapsack, his yellow eyes glow.

At five minutes before the bell, the loudspeaker crackles to life and the principal sets in with his announcements. A change in bus numbers. A lost sweater. Congratulations to fourth grader Lars Greevy on a successful appendectomy.

The minute hand finally kicks over to the hour. The bell rings, and Jenny charges into the hallway, running toward the main school door.

Her friend Dawn waits for her on the landing. Nose ring. Black lipstick. Deathly pallor. A spikey crop of royal blue hair.

Dawn has agreed to walk Jenny to the Metro stop. Dawn knows a short cut. She often sneaks out of her house and hops trains into town with her boyfriend, Ronnie, the juvenile offender.

The girls hustle down the loop to the street. They turn right into a housing project, cut up the driveway beside a split-level, and pass through a scrubby stand of woods to the backside of a shopping center.

"What did you tell your dad?" Dawn asks.

"That you were trying out for majorettes. That I was going along to watch."

Dawn laughs. Her tongue stud clatters against her incisors. "What if he calls me?" Dawn asks.

"He won't. I'll be back before he gets home."

"Who is this sick guy anyway?"

Jenny shrugs. "Just some guy. But he needs me. You'll see."

Dawn and Jenny pass out of the lot onto a busy Falls Church artery. They stop at an intersection, and Dawn points down along the next block.

"See it?"

Jenny picks out the pair of boxy Metroline beacons by the station stairway.

"Wish me luck."

As the girls hug, Dawn pokes and jostles Jenny's book bag. Roughly. Provocatively. The gullet distends. The jaws hinge open. The noise is sudden and piercing. Like steam from a pipe.

The platform is crowded at the center but largely deserted on either end. Jenny handles her book bag carefully as she makes her way to the far end of the platform where she seats herself on a bench. She settles the thing lightly onto her knees.

She is too preoccupied and nervous to notice him at first, even though he's just the sort of man her father has taught her to notice. He is grimy and shifty. He mutters to himself as he sorts through refuse in a trash can. He sees Jenny alone her bench, talking to her knapsack.

She only sees him once he has dropped down beside her on the bench. His funk is nearly overwhelming. She would ask him to leave her alone if she could draw breath enough to speak.

He leans in close. "Don't you say nothing," he tells her and relieves her of her book bag, snatching it violently off her lap.

He plunders through the outer pocket. He helps himself to Jenny's mints and both of her ballpoints.

"Mister," she manages lowly. "Mister, please don't."

Jenny feels the air in the station stir and surge as the D.C. bound metro approaches, pushing a draft before it through the tunnel.

"Mister, please," she says.

He sneers at her as he reaches deep into the main compartment of her bag. He draws out the pickle jar with the scarlet lizard scuttling about the bottom. It spins frantically. It lunges and darts, probing with its tongue.

"What in the living shit . . .?"

He is peering through a puncture in the jar lid as the scarlet lizard spits. Milky venom sprays into his eye. It splatters onto his cheek. His lips.

He lacks the will to shout, the strength to move. His muscles stiffen and contract. He quivers and quakes on the bench as the eastbound train rolls into the station.

Jenny snatches the jar from his shaking hand. She grabs her book bag and gains the edge of the platform just as the subway doors slide open.

Jenny looks out through a smudged window as the train departs the station. She sees him on the bench, quite still now. He sits stiffly with his legs thrown out before him. She tells herself he is only asleep.

With her laminated Metro map, Jenny follows their progress. Ballston. Virginia Square. Clarendon. Court House. Rosslyn.

She rises to stand before the doorway as they approach the Foggy Bottom-GWU stop. The doors slide open, and Jenny exits the train. She emerges from the station onto the street and peers about to get her bearings.

She is familiar with the route. It is the way they traveled when they visited her mother near the end. Taking the train. Walking the Mall. Talking. Her father trying to comfort and reassure her. Her father trying to make his little jokes. Her father trying not to cry.

Jenny shivers a little at the sight of the place with its brightly illuminated sign on the crown of the building --

The George Washington University Medical Center. She carefully works her arms through her book bag straps and sets out along the walk.

The lobby is swamped with visitors. It smells of lily of the valley and stale perfume. Jenny falls in line at the reception desk behind a woman with a tattered paper sack. A man with a bonzai tree.

She has developed a story. Jenny is prepared to perform as she steps to the desk to take her turn with the chunky receptionist in the pink cardigan.

Jenny looks her squarely in the eye, just as her father has taught her.

"Well, hello, sugar. What can I do for you?"

"We're here to see my grandpa. My mom's parking the car."

"And what's your grandpa's name?"

"Tillman. He's a senator."

The receptionist punches up the name on the screen.

"You'll have to see that girl over there, honey."

The receptionist points toward the Mellon Pavilion desk. Quarried slate. Polished marble. Ashley. No waiting.

Jenny crosses the lobby. She watches Ashley check her face in a compact mirror. Ashley has had her hair trimmed and styled. She has bought new shoes. She has worn a daringly clingy dress. She is consumed with the prospect of George Clooney. She looks anxiously toward the lobby doors each time they slide open.

Ashley fails at first to notice Jenny, who can barely see over the elegant counter.

Jenny clears her throat, and Ashley glances her way.

"Yes?" Her tone is curt. Businesslike.

"We're here to see my grandpa. My mom's parking the car."

Ashley manages a thin smile. "Let's wait for your mom to get here."

"She told me not to. She told me to go on up."

"Name?"

"Tillman. He's a senator."

Ashley is suddenly interested in Jenny. Keenly interested.

She leans toward Jenny. She speaks lowly, in a discreet whisper.

"Is your mom his daughter?"

Jenny nods.

"So she's parking the car?"

Jenny nods.

"Did she bring a . . .friend?"

Ashley draws closer still. She is nearly sprawled upon the polished marble desktop. Anxious for the answer.

Jenny adjusts accordingly.

"Uh huh," she says.

Ashley smiles. She stands upright and tugs at the hem of her brief, clingy dress.

"Your grandpa's on eight. Here, you can hold these."

Ashley slides a trio of tongue-oiled, Koa wood passes across the marble desktop.

"So they're coming right in?"

Jenny nods.

"How do I look?"

Ashley turns around to permit Jenny a full inspection.

"Your hair's kind of poofy in the back."

Ashley reaches up in a panic to smooth her tresses. She checks with Jenny, who shakes her head. "You might want to brush it."

Ashley snatches her purse from beneath the counter. "I'll be right back." She runs clattering in her heels into an alcove behind her desk and disappears into the toilet.

The hammered, bronze elevator doors slide shut upon Jenny. The car rises with a graceful whir into the Mellon Pavilion tower.

36

Doug has developed repartee. He has jotted on a pad of paper potential conversational topics. He has written and polished a number of wry remarks. He sits in the teachers' lounge rehearsing them. Lowly. Mrs. Dunleavy, the school nurse, has rolled down her stockings for comfort's sake and is sprawled upon the sofa, asleep.

Doug is supposed to be grading tests. A stack of them rests on the tabletop before him. His classes are finished for the day. He is just killing time before his trip into town. Before Beatrice.

"Beatrice," he says aloud.

He likes the sound of it. "Beatrice," he says again. This time suavely.

"Where?"

It's Janice. She has slipped up behind him. She holds her dingy, public-radio mug.

"Where'd you come from?"

"What's this?" Janice snatches up Doug's notepad before he can move to stop her. She scans it, shaking her head. She reads selections aloud.

"Mention new Getty museum. Italian restaurant in Manassas. Lasagna. Possible dinner."

Doug lunges and grabs the pad away from Janice. He shoves it and the stack of tests into his satchel. He gathers up his paper sack and accompanies Janice into the hallway.

"Should I tell her hair looks nice?"

"If it looks nice."

"It's just that I haven't had to talk to a woman in a long time."

"If that's a Barbara crack, I resent it."

"No, I mean a woman I like. A woman I want to make a good impression on."

"Dougie, just talk to her like you talk to me, and you'll be fine. And you know that story you like to tell about your trip to the Smokies?"

"The one with the bobcat?"

"Yeah, that one. Don't."

They walk in silence for a moment as Doug adjusts his repartee accordingly.

"Is this him?" Janice points to the paper sack in Doug's hand. Doug nods.

"Let me get one more look."

Doug hands over the paper sack to Janice.

"You know, Dougie," she says as she unrolls the throat of the sack, "a man with a special lizard doesn't really need small talk."

Janice pulls out a jar. It is quite empty. It isn't even a pickle jar. Janice peers into it.

"Now this *is* a special lizard," she says and shows the empty jar to Doug.

He takes the jar from her. Chunky Jiff. Straight from the kitchen. Spotlessly clean. No holes in the lid.

"Oh no," Doug says lowly, gravely. "Oh no."

Doug turns back along the corridor and fairly bolts toward the administrative office.

"Dougie!"

Jenny's friend Dawn lies sprawled on her bed reading a beauty magazine. She studies a layout devoted to a particularly bony model who looks like a heroine addicted vampire. Pale. Slight. Drawn. Desperate for a transfusion.

Dawn adores her purple nail polish. She is jotting down the make and hue as her telephone rings. She grabs the receiver and rolls onto her back. "Talk to me."

The voice on the line is adult. Stern.

"Yeah, this is Dawn."

As Dawn listens, she rolls back over on the bed. She sits up stiffly, nervously.

"Oh, Mr. Gunther. Hey."

37

Jenny reads the patients' names on their doors. Tillman. Tillman. Tillman. Jenny steps into a room to avoid a nurse. The TV plays. It's tuned to Stories of the Highway Patrol. The patient -- a frail, elderly woman -- lies unconscious in the bed.

Jenny slips back into the hallway once the coast is clear. She hears a man just down the hall. He moans and whimpers pathetically. "Sofferenza, sofferenza. La vendetta. Morte. Morte."

Jenny checks the name. Her guy all right. She slips into the room to find it empty but for Tillman.

Royce Tillman doesn't look much like a senator to Jenny. He squirms on the bed. He has kicked away the bed sheet. He wears a cotton bathrobe over his hospital gown, the gesture of a sympathetic nurse. His wrists are tethered to the bedrail. His hairpiece sits on the tray table beside his untouched lunch.

He seems wonderstruck by the sight of Jenny. Purely delighted. Tears roll down his cheeks. "Piccina! Piccina!"

Jenny eases toward the bed. She is used to her senators on the news. Blue suits. Flag lapel pins. Bombast. Tillman is frightening to look upon. He jerks against his tethers. He is musky-smelling. Rancid.

"Liberarmi, tesoro." Sweetheart, he calls her.

Jenny unzips her book bag and draws from it the pickle jar. Already, the scarlet lizard is frantic to escape. Twitching. Circling.

Tillman cries out at the sight of it. Jenny shuts the door. "Mia lucertola! Mio condottiero!"

Jenny tries to shush him with a finger to her lips. He is sobbing now. "Don't you worry. You're going to be just fine. You'll see."

Jenny unscrews the jar lid, and the scarlet lizard crawls out onto the bed. It mounts Tillman's leg and scurries up his torso. It stops upon his chest. It waits.

Tillman tugs at his tethers.

"Tesoro," he says sweetly, lowly, "liberarmi."

Jenny unties Tillman's wrists, freeing him to reach for the lizard. It crawls onto his open palm. Tillman covers it with his other hand and raises them to his face. His fingers are intertwined, as if in prayer.

Jenny watches, dumbfounded, as the first wisps of scarlet smoke drift toward the acoustical ceiling tile. The smoke thickens quickly. It billows and rises. Tillman inhales deeply, drawing a stream of it in through his nostrils. He rolls upright, placing his feet upon the floor.

Jenny rushes to the solitary window. She is laboring still to unlatch it and throw it open as the smoke detector goes off and the hospital fire alarm sounds. Jenny turns back to find Tillman gone. There is smoke, thick and scarlet, riding out against the ceiling. There is red ash littering the floor.

The corridors of the Mellon Pavilion are, immediately, studies in pandemonium. The alarm still sounds. Pulsing. Piercing. Friends and relatives of patients and patients themselves -- accustomed to privilege and special consideration -- demand answers of nurses and hospital officials.

They want to know what's burning. They want to know now.

Up on the eighth floor, lost in the furor, Jenny rushes into the hallway. She looks up and down its length. No Tillman. "Mister! Mister!"

At the near end of the corridor, Jenny notices the stairwell door swinging slowly shut.

Tillman looks like any other patient. Frail. Sickly. In fear of death by incineration. He moves stiffly down the stairs. He has descended four floors without pausing before he stops to draw open a landing door. Tillman gazes blankly into the corridor. Maternity. He lets the door swing shut and continues on. Descending.

Tillman enters the deserted second-floor hallway. Examination rooms. Out-patient treatment. The Mellon Pavilion's own plush brand of emergency medical care. The staff and patients have evacuated to the lobby and the street.

Tillman is quite alone. He walks stiffly and obliviously directly to the end of the corridor, as if he knows where he's going. He steps through the swinging doors of a treatment room.

There is an adjustable stainless-steel examination table with glove-leather padding and brass highlights in the center of the room. The walls are lined with cabinets and cupboards. Electronic monitors. A pair of Kandinsky reproductions.

Tillman yanks open drawers and spills their contents onto the floor. Syringes. Swabs. Tongue depressors. Bandages. Sealed, sterilized packets that clatter on the quarry tile floor.

Tillman takes up a packet. He yanks it open. It holds a gleaming scalpel, murderously sharp. He places it carefully on the examination table. He opens another packet. Tillman positions the second scalpel, with meticulous care, just alongside the first.

Jenny slips along a corridor in the maternity ward, peeking into the doorways. The fire alarm shuts off, and the sudden silence is unnerving. Jenny hears footsteps behind her. The jangling of keys.

"Mommy?" she says as she ducks into a room.

The guard continues past in his blue security uniform. He is white and blubbery, a little winded from his tour of the tower.

He enters the stairwell. Jenny peeks out in his wake. She continues along the hallway.

"Mister," she says in an urgent whisper. "Mister."

146

As the guard descends through the tower, he stops on each floor in turn. He's been sent to look for smoke or flame.

He reaches the second floor and exits the stairwell. The corridor is empty. The area, vacant.

"Anybody here?" he calls out.

No response.

"Hey! Anybody around!?"

The guard is set to return to the stairwell, has his hand upon the push bar when he is stopped by a metallic clatter down along the hallway.

"Hello!"

Nothing.

He strikes out along the corridor. He looks into each treatment and examination alcove he passes. He checks the restrooms. The supply rooms. The nurses' station.

Through the glass door light of a treatment room at the head of the hallway, he sees a man. A patient in a bathrobe. Bald. Sick. Old.

He pushes open the treatment room door.

"Okay, sir. Let's clear out. Didn't you hear the alarm?"

Tillman ignores him altogether. He has laid out dozens of scalpels on the examination table. They have been neatly placed in rows and columns. Each is identical to the next.

"Why don't we take you down stairs. Let's go. You ought not to be in here."

Tillman selects his weapon. He plucks it from the middle of the table. He lays the blade of it to his left thumb. He easily finds bone. He bleeds freely.

"Jesus! What did you go and do that for!?"

Disgusted and incensed, the guard closes on Tillman and grabs at his arm.

"Give me that damn thing!"

Tillman resists. Not violently, but stoutly and steadfastly. The guard reaches for the scalpel.

147

"Give it here."

"Si ferma!"

The guard struggles with Tillman, clutches at his arm.

"Hand it over!"

"Si ferma!"

Tillman jerks free of the guard's grip. With a quick, slashing motion, Tillman whips the blade across the guard's neck. The edge is so sharp and precisely machined that the cut is impeccably clean and nearly imperceptible.

"Shit!" the guard says, already with a moist gurgle.

He looks surprised. A little sheepish. Blood seeps from the razor-thin wound across his neck. It quickly thickens to a steady flow. The guard sinks to his knees. He collapses to the floor.

Tillman--scalpel in hand, his thumb dripping blood--steps over him and into the hallway. He enters the stairwell and descends.

38

Doug veers to the curb before the National Gallery and comes to a skidding stop. He charges into the vaulted foyer and runs over to the coat-check counter. There is a girl there. Twentyish. Unoccupied but for her gum.

"I'm looking for Beatrice Malloy. She works here."

The girl gazes at him blankly. She is not responsible for information. She only hangs up coats. She says nothing. She can't even be bothered to shrug.

Doug dashes across the rotunda floor and into the gallery proper. He looks around a little hopelessly. Tourists. Rubens. A guard holding up a doorframe. Doug hurries over to him.

"I'm looking for Beatrice Malloy."

Stupefied and numb from a shift's worth of watching people watch paintings, the guard is slow to respond. "Who?" he finally says.

"Beatrice Malloy. She's some kind of conservator. Do you know her?"

The guard is still only gazing blankly as Doug hears from behind, "Beatrice?"

He turns to see a man standing just behind him. Squat. Plain. Bespectacled. Howard.

"Yeah," Doug says. "Do you know where I can find her?"

Howard subjects Doug to comprehensive study. "Who wants to know?"

Ted and Beatrice sit in her cluttered office plotting a museum purchase. A Titian from a private collector in a severe real estate bind.

149

"Squeeze him," Ted says. "He's stuck for money, and we've got a roomful of Titians already."

"What if he goes to the Met?"

"He won't. You know the sort. Super-patriot. Democratic fat cat. He'll want it to be here, so he can show it off when he's in town.

"Offer him half?"

"At most."

"Beatrice?" Beatrice looks to see Amy standing in the office doorway. "A Mr. Gunther here to see you," Amy says.

Doug squeezes past Amy into the office.

"Doug, hi. I'm still kind of in the middle of . . ."

"We've got a problem." As Doug speaks, he produces the empty peanut butter jar from the sack in his hand."

"Where is he?"

"Jenny took him?"

"To school?"

Doug shakes his head. "To Tillman," he says.

A side hospital door swings open. Tillman steps into the afternoon sunlight onto Twenty-Third Street. He is shoeless in the cool spring air. He looks like an elderly street urchin. His bathrobe is splattered with blood. He walks south. Stiffly. Slowly. Resolutely. Tillman has traveled nearly two blocks by the time the door swings open again and Jenny steps onto the walk. It takes a moment for her eyes to adjust from the gloom of the stairwell. She looks north. Nothing. She peers south, craning to see past oncoming pedestrians.

The cotton robe. The bare legs.

She runs after him.

"Mister?"

He is oblivious. Deaf to her.

"Mister!?"

Jenny catches up with Tillman and moves along beside him, talking to him. His gaze is glassy and fixed. Blood drips from his sliced thumb. Onto his robe. Onto his foot. Onto the D.C. sidewalk.

"You're hurt." Jenny tugs at his bathrobe sleeve. "Let's go back and get you fixed up."

Tillman stops. He turns toward Jenny.

Only now does she see the scalpel in his other hand. He jabs it at her, slicing the air. The blade passes just beneath Jenny's chin. She leaps and dodges out of reach.

"Mister!"

"Piccina," Tillman says lowly, grimly. "Morte. Morte."

She doesn't need to speak Italian. From his eyes, from the ruthless edge on the scalpel, she takes his meaning.

Tillman turns back and continues, carefully placing one foot in front of the other.

"But . . .Mister!"

He must go.

"Mister!"

Jenny trails along behind him, calling from time to time. She looks about for a policeman. One sails through the intersection ahead of her, eastbound on F in a radio car. She shouts and waves, but he doesn't see her.

"Mister!" she calls again, a little forlornly now. She wishes she'd gone straight home. She really really wishes she'd gone straight home.

"Mister, please!"

Tillman fails to answer. He no longer looks her way. He only walks. Slowly. Glassy-eyed. He only bleeds.

Ashley sees them running toward her. The man is agitated. Nearly frantic. The woman looks familiar and, Ashley notices, quite stunningly overhauled.

"Has a little girl been here?" Beatrice asks. "She's maybe this high. Brown hair."

151

Ashley studies Beatrice.

"Aren't you . . .?"

Beatrice nods. "Have you seen here?"

"The girl, have you seen her."

"Yeah, but I don't know where she went."

Beatrice grabs Doug by the hand. "Come on." She charges with him toward the hammered bronze elevator doors.

"Hey!" Ashley calls after them. "What about George?"

The excitement of the fire alarm has died away. The patients and visitors have returned to their rooms. Beatrice leads Doug into Tillman's room. It is empty. The bed is vacant.

Doug picks up the perforated lid of the pickle jar from Tillman's tray table and shows it to Beatrice. Together they watch a curious scrap of red ash blow and drift about the floor.

Downstairs in the outpatient and emergency treatment unit, a nurse has fallen. She has entered an examination room and lost her footing. Her legs have slipped from beneath her. She has dropped hard upon her side and has gotten the wind knocked from her.

She has noticed that the floor is wet and sticky. She has seen that it is pooled with blood. She has shifted about to find a dead security guard just beside her.

His neck has been cleanly sliced open. His wound gapes wide. His severed windpipe is exposed.

She finds the breath to scream.

39

It is the only precinct house Beatrice knows. It's located just north of the Capitol near Union Station. She was there once with Ted, the evening he found a young man trying to steal his precious Saab.

Ted had confronted him while armed exclusively with indignation. The young man had a screwdriver. A hammer. Knuckles. An officer was kind to them. His name was Roark. Beatrice finally gets the attention of the sergeant at the precinct desk.

"Is Officer Roark here?" Beatrice asks him.

The sergeant shakes his head. Something I can help you with?"

"We've got sort of a problem."

A detective enters from the street. Jessup. He is black and pushing sixty. Heavy-set. He stops by the desk for his messages. He sorts through the jumble of slips laid out on the desktop.

Beatrice leans toward the sergeant. She speaks to him softly, discreetly. "It's sort of delicate and involves a senator."

Detective Jessup glances at Beatrice and Doug. At the sergeant.

"Which one?" Jessup asks.

"Royce Tillman. We think he's . . . a danger to himself and others."

"Go on," Jessup tells her.

"We think he's going to kill somebody," Beatrice says.

"And he's got my girl?" Doug adds.

Jessup shoots a look at the sergeant, a sort of what-the-hell-did-I-walk-into glance. Detective Jessup

153

motions for Beatrice and Doug to follow, and he leads them into the detectives' squad room, which, even by Beatrice's standards, is breathtakingly cluttered.

"Sit," Jessup says as he sweeps police forms off a pair of metal chairs, raining them onto the floor. He takes a seat behind a desk, which is heaped with files.

"Now," he says, "what's up with Tillman?"

Beatrice and Doug look uneasily at each other. She begins.

"He's . .uh . . sick."

"Sick how?"

"He's . . . unhinged."

"The man's a friend of yours?"

Doug and Beatrice shake their heads.

"Then how does your kid know him?"

"She doesn't," Doug says. "Not really. She just heard he was sick. She wanted to . . . . help him."

"And now he's going to kill somebody?" Jessup asks.

Beatrice nods. "Probably with a knife."

"And your girl's with him?"

Doug nods. "She went to see him at the hospital."

"GWU?" Jessup asks.

Doug nods.

Jessup turns toward a wiry, fidgeting detective at an adjacent desk. He is plowing through a stack of paperwork.

"Something over at GWU, wasn't there?

"A guard." The detective runs his finger across his neck. "Ear to ear. Maybe an hour ago."

Tillman moves slowly west along the Mall. He passes between the Vietnam Memorial and the reflecting pool. Jenny follows some twenty yards behind him.

"Mister," she says with a quivering whimper. "Mister."

He strides slowly on, oblivious to her. He must go.

154

Tillman crosses 17th Street, wading full into traffic. Cars veer and skid to avoid him. Drivers blow their horns and swear. As Tillman clears the roadway, he climbs the gentle slope toward the Washington Monument. Jenny follows.

She sees a man in a tan uniform. She thinks he is some sort of law officer. She waves her arms to get his attention. "Hey," she calls, "Help me."

He is a marine master sergeant. He has wandered out of a bar on 19th Street.

"Hey!"

A little girl waves her arms at him. Even in his bourbon-induced haze, he feels relatively certain that he doesn't know any little girls in the district.

"Help me!" she calls.

He lurches over to see what the trouble is. Her explanation is complicated. Something about her friend -- a bald, old coot in a bathrobe.

"Don't you worry, sugar. The marines have landed." The master sergeant winks at Jenny over his shoulder as he closes on Tillman. "Hey, buddy," he says and lays his hand to Tillman's shoulder.

Tillman stops. He turns slowly to face the master sergeant.

"Morte," Tillman says and probes with his scalpel through the master sergeant's starched shirt. He pricks him again. And again. The blade passes easily through flesh. Between ribs. There is but the slightest, stinging pain.

"Ouch." The master sergeant covers his wounds with his hands. Blood soaks through is shirt. Drips from his fingers. He lurches away from Tillman. Away from Jenny who chases after him, trying to help.

"Mister," she says. "Mister."

The master sergeant lurches toward 19th Street, suddenly persuaded he should have never left the bar.

40

Jack Proctor has passed through his customary stages of inebriation. First there was his bitter and poisonously articulate stage. He was generous with insults. Pam packed up and stormed out in tears. Lewis threatened him with bodily harm, but jokingly and while wearing his dopey grin.

Jack dialed Delores Tillman to tell her about the photographs. She let him rail and complain. Then, when she finally spoke, she only asked him one question: "How did I look?"

By the time Jack has drained the fifth of Johnny Walker, he has passed into feverish psychosis. He sits at his desk and mutters bitterly. He breaks his empty scotch bottle on the marble top of his credenza. He opens his office window and shouts down to the street. Blue profanity. A few people glance up, but most just ignore him.

He sends Lewis out for a bottle of Famous Grouse.

Lewis returns to find Jack Proctor weepy and sentimental. He blubbers to Lewis about his secret love for the first lady's press secretary. He breaks into a ballad from the Gloria Estefan songbook. He lapses into a bit of late Cher. It leads to Aretha.

"Come on," he tells Lewis.

"Where are we going?"

"Capitol. Rotunda," Proctor says.

"Why?"

"Why!? Proctor stumbles through his office doorway, his bottle of Grouse raised high above his head. "Because, my young man, the acoustics are splendid!"

This is not what Lewis had in mind. When he submitted three years' worth of applications. When he took the bus from Lexington. When he passed that first, nervous night in his dumpy studio apartment off Connecticut.

This is not what Lewis had in mind at all.

41

Ted licks his thumb and rubs a scuff mark from his saddle-leather briefcase as he crosses to the main National Gallery entranceway. Out on the landing, he examines his case for further signs of rough use.

It was a gift from Duane after a tiff. It was ludicrously expensive. Ted has visited the store where it was purchased. Ted has priced it himself. Duane inspects it every evening. Conspicuously. Rigorously.

Ted smoothes out a patch of raised hide with oil from the palm of his hand. As he descends the sweeping front stairway to Constitution Avenue, Ted looks about for Beatrice and Doug. No sign of them still.

Ted decides to swing by GWU and look for them there. The Marquis di Laguna. A return engagement.

He walks west to 7th Street and south into the Mall. He has been blessed this day by the parking gods. A fine spot near a corner. Convenient. Safe.

Ted's precious Saab has not been dinged or bumped, as best he can tell. He finds no marks from trouser rivets. No bird droppings. Ted depresses the button on his key fob, and his parking lights blink at him. His coupe beeps and coos. He opens the passenger door and gently settles his briefcase onto the seat.

As he circles his Saab, Ted sifts through his keys for the one to the Club on his steering wheel. The ring slips from his fingers and drops to the pavement.

He kicks it inadvertently to the gutter where it hangs up momentarily on the ribs of a steel rain grate before falling through and disappearing from sight.

"NO!!" Ted peers into the grate. He gives an agonized groan. Murky darkness and a swampy funk.

Ted glances about the Mall. Exasperated. Hoping for help. He sees a woman with a retriever. He sees scores of joggers. Assorted tourists consulting maps. He sees a bald man in what looks like a bathrobe. He is followed by a little girl.

Ted is on his hands and knees. Ted is poking into the gutter with a stick when he stops suddenly. He frees his twig to drop into the drainpipe. Ted stands. A bald man, he thinks, in a bathrobe? A little girl?

He scans for them and finds them again. They are opposite the Air and Space Museum. Tillman. He walks slowly and deliberately, as if he has only just learned how. His robe is blood-stained about the hem. The late afternoon sun glints off the blade of the scalpel in Tillman's right hand.

The girl follows, well back and out of reach.

"Was it . . . Jenny?" Ted says to himself, trying the name.

Ted actively regrets that he is not courageous. He would like nothing better than to dart across the Mall and rescue Doug Gunther's daughter. Disarm Royce Tillman. Maybe even pummel him a little on behalf of his brother sodomites. But Ted only twitches and whimpers instead. He takes a few tentative steps across the walk in the general direction of the Mall.

"Oh, God!" he says with a moan as he sets out in earnest toward Tillman. "Oh, God."

Ted plucks his cell phone from his jacket pocket as he advances across the mall. He punches in 911.

"Emergency operator," he hears over the line.

Ted draws a deep breath and swallows hard.

"Ma'am," he says, "This is complicated, so bear with me."

They roll in Detective Jessup's Chevy south along 23rd Street. Beatrice rides in the front with Jessup. Doug is in the back. The windows are smudged. The upholstery stinks. Doug is queasy now, on top of being frantic with worry.

Jessup has dispatched officers to search the hospital while they scour the neighboring streets in his sedan.

"What's she wearing?" Jessup asks over his shoulder.

"I don't remember."

"Pants? Dress? Stripes? Checks?"

Doug gets a flash on the frilly dress. The girlish shoes.

"A dress! That's right. I think it had flowers on it."

Jessup's cell phone chirps in his coat pocket. He fishes it out and takes the call.

"Yeah."

Doug and Beatrice study the pedestrians along the walk. Adults. Skirts and sneakers. Sweat pants. Charcoal suits. Ashen complexions.

"A marine?" Jessup says. "Where exactly?" Jessup listens with an expression on his face that grows more perplexed by the moment. "Hold on a second."

He takes the phone from his ear and turns to Beatrice. "Have you got some nutcase friend named Ted?"

Ted follows the little girl who follows Tillman. Ted only watches at first. He says nothing. He eases gradually closer to the pair of them.

"Jenny," he tries, saying it in a whisper.

She doesn't hear him.

"Jenny," he hisses.

Tillman stops. He lifts his head. He almost appears to be sniffing the air.

"Jenny," Ted says again, louder now. Jenny hears him and turns. "I'm a friend of your dad's," he tells her. "A friend of Beatrice's. You know Beatrice, don't you?"

Jenny nods.

Ted motions with his hand. "Come on over here. Away from him."

As Ted points toward him, Tillman turns. He looks at Ted. He smiles.

Ted grins as best he's able. "Evening, Senator," he says.

"Ah," Tillman tells him, "signore."

Tillman steps toward Ted. He raises the scalpel. "Per i suoi delitti."

"Run!" Jenny yelps. "He already stabbed a guy!" Jenny charges toward Ted. She grabs his hand and pulls him along. "Run!"

Ted backs away from Tillman who advances steadily. "No," Ted tells Tillman. "Not me."

Tillman presses forward.

Jenny tugs at Ted. "Mister!"

"I'm not your guy!" Ted screams at Tillman as, finally, Ted breaks into a jog, holding to Jenny's hand. They run east along the Mall toward the Capitol. "I'm from Indianapolis!" Ted shouts over his shoulder.

Tillman -- his scalpel upraised, a smile on his lips -- follows. He accelerates -- walking still, but faster now. Crisply and with resolve.

"Ah," he says again. "Signore."

42

Lewis stands at the portico doors of the United States Capitol building looking west along the Mall. The view makes for a glorious vista in the late afternoon sun. Ordinarily Lewis would be filled with pride, would possibly even be a little teary. Instead, he is merely sorry he ever left Lexington. He beats his forehead against the door light while, from the rotunda, Jack Proctor sings.

"Bang, bang. She shot me down. Bang, bang. That awful sound."

On second thought, Lewis believes he might just cry after all.

"Bang, bang. I hit the ground. Bang, bang. My baby shot me down."

A black security guard passes through the rotunda on his rounds. He has checked already Jack Proctor's Senatorial credentials. He has tried already to tempt Jack Proctor to leave the rotunda and go back to his office.

Proctor interrupts his singing. He raises his fist. "What up, bro'," he says.

The guard only shakes his head as he continues through to join Lewis at the portico doors.

"You can't do nothing with him!? How's this going to look if my boss comes through here."

"He's bound to give out," Lewis says. "I mean he's just got to. That's his second bottle of scotch."

"It's a wonder this damn government ever gets anything done."

There's suddenly static and a voice from the guard's radio in the holster on his hip. The talk is garbled and broken. The guard keys the handset. "I'll be around in a minute."

"Just get him gone some way or another," the guard tells Lewis. "We're closing in ten, and I don't want to have to fool with him."

"I'll try," Lewis says.

Grumbling still, the guard leaves the portico on his rounds. Lewis, left alone, returns to thumping his forehead against the door light.

Glancing back over his shoulder, Ted whimpers at the sight of Tillman. The blood-stained robe. The upraised scalpel. The unnerving smile.

"Oh God," he says, near tears.

Jenny pulls him along, running with Ted east along the Mall.

"Have you got a car?"

Ted nods.

"Where is it?"

Ted points vaguely west along the Mall.

"But I lost my keys!" Ted blubbers a little as he speaks.

He looks again toward Tillman who presses ahead steadily. Tillman crosses Fourth Street behind them. Third Street. He follows them up Maryland Avenue toward the Capitol. He is forty yards back, but they can't seem to pull away.

He grins at them. "Ah," he says from time to time, "Signore."

"Listen to me," Ted tells Jenny. "Listen. My dad's people come from the U.P.. They're German. My Mom's from Galveston. He can't want me. It's some kind of mistake."

Ted glances back again. Tillman still follows – bloody, maniacal, dogged. "Oh God!" Ted says in quivering whisper.

Jenny leads Ted past the Garfield memorial toward a lower crypt door of the Capitol. "Help," she calls out to no one in particular. "Help us."

163

Only then does she see the young man in the handsome, moss green suit. He rhythmically pounds his head against a portico door.

43

Jessup rolls to a stop on Seventh Street, just where it bisects the Mall. He, Beatrice, and Doug climb out of the sedan.

"Jenny!" Doug shouts. Doug whistles. He peers west along the Mall. North toward the Ellipse and the White House. "Jenny!"

No sign of her, but two retrievers and an Irish Setter run toward Doug along the Mall with their owners in shrieking pursuit.

It is Jessup who sees him. Jessup who calmly and carefully surveys the Mall. Up and back. Down and across. West toward the Capitol, just past the reflecting pool, he sees a guy in bathrobe. Bald. Shoeless. Pantless even.

"Hey," he says and points. "What about him?"

Beatrice cups her hands to her mouth. "Si ferma!" she shouts. Stop.

Tillman pauses briefly. He turns. Failing afternoon sunlight glints off his freckled scalp. Off the blade of the scalpel in his hand.

Doug is running before Jessup can stop him. "Hey!" Doug shouts as Tillman turns back toward the Capitol. "Hey!" he shrieks as Tillman strides ahead.

Jack Proctor flings his empty Grouse bottle and sends it skidding across the polished, marble floor of the rotunda.

"Where the eagles fly," he sings in a slurred, groggy voice, "in the clear blue sky." He hears voices to his right, toward the portico. They are loud. Thoughtless.

165

"I'm singing here!"

Lewis rubs his forehead as he listens to them. He looks them over. A little girl. A frantic man.

"He wants to kill me!" Ted says.

"He does," Jenny adds and nods.

"We need a cop or something. Somebody! You've got to help us." Ted clutches at Lewis's Armani suit.

"Who wants to kill you?" Lewis asks as he tries to pull away from Ted. There is a touch of the Godless sodomite about him. Lewis can tell.

"Tillman, that lunatic!"

"Royce Tillman?" Lewis asks.

"Ah," he hears, "signore."

Royce Tillman stands at the mouth of the stairwell in his blood-stained bathrobe. He strides forward, his bare feet silent on the stone floor. Lewis can't believe his eyes.

"Senator Tillman?" he says.

"Oh God!" is all Ted can manage as he backs with Jenny across the floor.

The security guard, making his rounds, charges out of the rotunda toward Lewis.

"What did I tell you!" he barks at him, but Lewis only points. The guard looks to see some old, bald coot in a bathrobe. He drips blood onto the polished marble floor.

"For shit's sake, what is going on here!?" the guard shouts. "You're bleeding on my floor," he says as he steps toward Tillman. "And where are your damn shoes? This is the United States Capitol, in case you didn't know."

Only then does he see the scalpel, just as it is raised and jabbed with a probing flick. The guard instinctively lifts his arm for protection. The blade enters at his wrist. It glances off bone with a clear, metallic ping.

"No!" Lewis shouts. "Senator!"

Lewis charges Tillman and wraps his arms around him. The guard is yelping already into his radio.

166

Tillman hardly feels sickly to Lewis. He is wiry and strong. Lewis struggles with him across the portico. He gets sudden, violent, unanticipated help from Ted who charges across the portico to fling himself into the fray.

The three of them stumble into the rotunda and fall to the floor just in front of Jack Proctor. He watches a man in a bathrobe probe once with the brief blade of his silver knife. There in the soft flesh, just between Lewis'ribs.

"That must smart," Proctor says.

Lewis glances at him and groans as Proctor studies the man in the bathrobe. He looks familiar to Proctor through his alcohol haze.

"Royce?" Proctor says, "is that you?"

Ted crawls and paws and scratches his way across the floor with Tillman scrabbling along behind him. This is his Jesse Helms' nightmare all over again, but for real.

"Royce, you miserable son-of-a-bitch!" Jack Proctor screams. Ted sees him rise to his feet, holding for support to a rotunda column. "Look what you've done!" Proctor shrieks. "You bastard! You've ruined everything!"

Jack Proctor charges toward Royce Tillman. He stumbles and drops heavily on top of him.

"Ho un' incarico!" Tillman wails.

"Speaka da English, asshole!" Proctor wallops Tillman with a crushing right. He laughs. Tillman slashes with the scalpel blade and lays open Proctor's forearm. Proctor laughs even louder, numb with scotch. He draws back his fist and breaks Tillman's nose.

"Dougie!"

Doug looks toward the Capitol. On the balcony, before the portico, he sees her. A little of her anyway above the railing. She is waving her arms.

"Dougie!" Jenny screams.

Raw adrenalin carries him up the stairs and into the portico where Jenny throws herself into her dad's arms.

The guard lies bleeding on the rotunda floor, holding his gashed wrist. Doug hears the struggle in the rotunda.

"Stay here, sweetie."

Doug dashes squarely into the bloodbath. A young man lies wounded on the floor, stabbed and bleeding. Tillman struggles still towars Ted as Proctor pummels him. Rides him. Berates him. Proctor is cut and bloody himself. He is conspicuously drunk.

Tillman's face is a gory mask. Blood flows from both nostrils. His thumb drips onto the marble floor.

"Doug!" It's Ted, his back now against the rotunda wall. "Help me!"

Tillman makes a desperate jab at Proctor, piercing him in the gut and bucking him from his back. Without thinking, Doug charges to take Proctor's place. He throws himself at Tillman. He struggles with him for the scalpel.

Doug grabs Tillman's wrist. He beats Tillman's hand against the marble floor and jars the scalpel free. It slides across the polished stone. Tillman crawls relentlessly after it.

Doug is clutching and pulling at Tillman as Proctor leaps onto Doug's back. He claws at Doug. He punches him. "Leave him alone!" he shrieks. "This asshole's mine!"

A body lands heavily on the three of them. The flowing hair. The fragrance. The handsome mauve dress. Beatrice flails away at Tillman, punching like a bantam-weight. She yells in his face. "Basta! Si ferma!"

Tillman crawls, dragging her as Doug tries to shed Proctor. Tillman closes on Ted. On the scalpel. He reaches for it. He strains for it. He almost has it.

A black, rubber-soled oxford stomps firmly upon Tillman's wrist, pinning it in place. With the toe of his other shoe, Jessup kicks the scalpel. It skids and clatters clear across the rotunda into the portico. Out of sight.

"That's about enough of this," Jessup says as he gives Tillman a stout tap to the cranium with the but of his pistol.

Tillman moans and collapses. He rolls onto his back. Beatrice straddles him. She slaps him hard across the face. "Si ferma!" she screams at him. "Basta!" Enough.

She slaps him again. Again.

The first wisps of smoke are slight and vaguely pink. They thicken. They deepen in color. They escape from every orifice and pore until Tillman looks to be smoldering. It is smoke without heat. Without odor. Bloody scarlet.

It gathers in a vivid plume as it drifts and rises into the murky reaches of the domed rotunda ceiling.   "What in the name of shit . . ." Jessup says, gazing into the dome.

Beatrice feels a stirring beneath her. A stiffening. Tillman gives a slight thrust at the hips. Beatrice hears a dry chuckle.

She looks down to find Tillman smirking. Aroused. He winks. "Hello, sugar," he says.

She wants it. He can tell. He can always tell.

44

There is bite to the night air. The sky is cloudless and littered with stars. Jenny, Beatrice, and Ted take in the splendid view of the Mall from the balcony of the west Capitol portico.

Behind them, inside, a half-dozen, uniformed metro cops mill about. Rescue-squad medics tend to Lewis and the wounded guard. To Proctor and Tillman.

Detective Jessup quizzes the senator, note pad in hand. He chews on his pen. He jots nothing.

Doug steps out onto the balcony. Jenny stands just before Beatrice. She leans upon her, chilled. Beatrice gathers Jenny beneath her coat flaps. Collects her in her arms.

"Jessup wants to talk to you," Doug tells Beatrice. "Somehow he thinks he might need a little help with his report."

"Is everybody going to be okay?"

Doug nods. "The drunk guy got the worst of it, but he can't feel it."

"What about Tillman?"

"He doesn't remember anything. One minute he's on the Mall getting his picture taken, and the next thing he knows he's in his housecoat in the Capitol."

"So he's going to be okay? Jenny asks.

"I guess," Doug tells her. "Is this thing ever going to end? This curse? Or does it just go on forever?"

Beatrice shrugs. "There's some hokum about a princess of Murano. You know, some descendent of Falieri's bride who finds her true love. The usual rubbish."

Ted pipes in. "So you're fine with magical lizards, but true love is hard to swallow?"

Beatrice smiles. She shrugs.

"I'm hungry." Jenny tugs at Doug's sleeve.

"Yeah," Doug says. "I could eat."

"What about you?" Beatrice pokes Ted with her elbow. He gazes distractedly out into the night sky.

"Who can eat? Don't you see, everything's different now. I've gone through my whole life thinking I'm from Indiana, and now this."

"Teddy, sweetheart," Beatrice says and kisses him on the cheek, "you are from Indiana."

They walk west along Constitution toward Ted's precious Saab. Jenny holds Beatrice's hand. Ted vows to learn Italian. Thoroughly. Fluently. The tongue of his people, he calls it.

They reach the car and stand waiting for Ted to unlock the doors. He feels about his pockets for his keys. His befuddled expression yields to a wan, sheepish grin as he recalls exactly where they are.

Ted wedges his forefinger between his teeth and bites the flesh theatrically. "Accidenti!" he says.

45

The senatorial primary in Kentucky is a lively affair. Senator Royce Tillman competes for his seat against the sitting lieutenant governor, a man named Mitchell.

Mitchell is decent and honest, but untried on the national level. He is given to spontaneous acts of charity and compassion. He is sincere in his politics. He is unapologetically bald. He is quite dull and unengaging.

By comparison, Senator Royce Tillman is remarkably colorful. He has recovered from a debilitating bout of Asian brain fever. An imported virus. Just the sort of thing that, with the aid of the voters, he would help keep from our shores.

Tillman's wife, Delores, joins him at campaign stops to gaze fondly upon him, kiss him chastely on the lips, hold tightly to his hand.

Senator Royce Tillman has killed a man in his Asian brain fever delirium, but the Lord has forgiven him for it. The man's widow has forgiven him for it. She routinely joins Royce and Delores on the dais to weep with them before the flag.

From either side of the stage, nightly and with unswerving vigor, Lewis and Jack Proctor lead the applause.

It is a sort of a honeymoon for them. The three of them. The service was small and private. Janice wept uncontrollably. Ted and Duane sniped at each other in hissed whispers. Beatrice's mother could hardly stop grinning. A son-in-law and a granddaughter, both at once!

After the vows were taken, they lingered in the chapel. Chatting. Snapping pictures. Sweetly and without prompting, Jenny threw her arms around Beatrice and kissed her on the cheek.

"Beety," she said.

They landed in Venice on a gray, foggy afternoon and hired a water taxi to carry them to their hotel. Across the lagoon. Past Murano. Into the Rio di San Giustina that bisects the city.

There was just the low hum of the inboard as they traveled along the narrow canal. Through the mist. Between the lurching rows of stuccoed buildings in their tumbledown antiquity.

With a blast of his horn, their driver swung them into the San Marco basin. Jenny, quite audibly, gasped.

Gondolas. Barges. Vaporetti. The twin columns on the molo. The teeming tourists. The delicate, pink, moorish facade of the Palazzo Ducale.

They have eaten tiny, tender calamaretti at Da Fiore. Razor clams at La Corte Sconta. Pastries at Cafe Florian. They have followed Beatrice through the cramped, winding alleyways of the city into gloriously sun washed campos. They have waded in the Adriatic. They have visited Beatrice's whiskery uncle on Murano.

They have purchased, finally, tickets to the doge's palace. They have toured the armory. The prison. They have crossed the Bridge of Sighs. They stand in the massive council chamber looking up at the veiled painting of Marino Falieri.

"It's Latin," Beatrice says. "'Here is the place of Marino Falieri, beheaded for his crimes'."

"Doesn't look like much from here, does it?" Doug says as he gazes toward the ceiling.

Jenny tugs at Doug's hand.

"Please, Daddy."

She has discovered gelato. There is a stand on the Rialto. The vendor knows her name.

"Okay, okay. Here we go."

They leave the council chamber. They move along a vaulted corridor and out onto the Giants' Stairway. They descend into the courtyard below. It is just as Doug remembers from his dream. The massive statuary. The carved railings. The tiles pitched and sloped toward an ancient stone grate.

Doug would like to peer into the drain, but Jenny grabs him. She tugs at him.

"Daddy, please!"

"Go on," he tells her. "We're coming."

Jenny runs ahead, through the gateway and into the piazza.

Doug smiles at Beatrice. He takes her face in his hands. He kisses her.

Arm in arm, the walk through the porta della carta and into the sun-drenched plaza beyond.

A Japanese tourist in the cavernous council chamber is the first to notice. He points, speechless.

The paint on the veiled portrait of the Doge Marino Falieri bubbles and blisters. It liquifies and runs in streaks down the polished marble chamber wall. A hushed and reverential silence falls upon the room.

Paint melts and drains from the canvas until it is virtually scoured and unmarked. An aged and parchment yellow. As if it has never seen the first speck of pigment. The first stroke of a brush.

Deep in the drain of the palace courtyard, along a fractured length of clay pipe, scarlet lizards are piled thick upon each other. They clot the way. Their yellow eyes glow. They smolder.

The smoke thickens and billows as the creatures go to ash. A scarlet plume boils out of the grate and wafts up the Giants' Stairway. A uniformed guard on the upper balcony shouts with alarm. "Fuoco!"

As Doug, Beatrice, and Jenny board a vaporetto on the Riva, carabinieri run into the Piazza. From the east along the fondamenta. From the north beyond the clock tower. They blow their whistles to clear the way. They dash toward the ornate gateway of the Palazzo Ducale. It boils with gaudy scarlet smoke.

Beatrice and Jenny and Doug stand at the rail of the water bus. Oblivious to the tumult behind them, they look out across the lagoon. They admire the Redentore. They debate restaurants for dinner.

The vaporetto warps away from it mooring and swings out into the chop. It chugs west across the San Marco Basin. Away up the Grand Canal.

fine